CW00673092

BROKEN MOON

CATE CASSIDY

RED SHORE PUBLISHING

Broken Moon

Wolves of Thunder Cove

Cate Cassidy

Broken Moon © 2021, Cate Cassidy

CHAPTER ONE

EMBER

The sun was quickly fading, and as the evening shadows appeared, my spine stiffened with uncertainty.

I'd left three men behind to chase down the ghosts of my past, to discover who I was and what clan I belonged to.

But as we forged on, headed toward unfamiliar territory, with nothing but the darkness ahead, I couldn't help but wonder if the past I was desperate to uncover would be my downfall. If it would destroy me.

I couldn't seem to shake the heavy feeling that wrapped itself around me. As we moved farther away from Thunder Cove, the stronger it got.

When I'd seen the horde fast approaching, I knew I needed to warn Grayson, Alex, and Cody. But then Rylen tackled me to the ground before I could. All I'd wanted to do was protect them.

It was the same reason I'd left.

But then Dawson had appeared, reaching out a hand and setting me back on solid ground with the promise he was bringing me home to my clan, my true family.

"How did you find me?"

It was the first time I'd spoken to him as we headed toward the portal together, his army of men and wolves close behind. I'd been deep in thought, and he'd seemed to sense that I needed time to process everything.

Dawson glanced at me briefly, a trace of a smile gracing his lips. "Word travels fast when a halfling is brought into our world. As soon as I heard, I knew it was you."

"And you knew because of the energy between us when you shook my hand?"

He was silent for a beat, his heavy boots squishing into the soft dirt beneath our feet.

"At the time, all I knew was you were a shifter but your wolf was dormant. I could feel her, though she was weak." He cleared his throat. "But when we touched, and we felt that connection, I was sure you were a member of my clan. You had to be."

I furrowed my brow. "But you didn't say anything."

He side-eyed me and smirked. "And what would you have done if a stranger had told you that you're a shifter and you needed to leave the world you knew for one you didn't?"

"Point taken," I replied.

"I did try to warn you, though." He shrugged. "I was pulled back into my realm before I could do anything else. I hoped you'd heard me."

I thought back to the night the dark creature had attacked me in the forest just outside the carnival grounds. The whisper in the darkness, telling me to look for the portal, telling me I didn't belong in the human world.

It seemed like forever ago, even though it hadn't been long at all. So much had happened in such a short time. Not only did I end up in a world where wolves and other shifters existed, but I'd discovered that I was one myself.

"That was you?"

He stopped walking and turned to me. "So, you heard me?"

I nodded. "You told me to look for the portal."

His face brightened. "I did, and I'm happy you listened. The idea of you staying in the human world left me with many sleepless nights."

He resumed his brisk pace. I did my best to keep up with him, but his long legs were starting to pose a problem.

"I didn't have a chance to listen, but none of that matters now. I'm here."

I didn't elaborate, and thankfully, he didn't ask me to. I knew I'd have to explain at some point that a wolf slayer had attacked and marked me, but it didn't feel like the right time. He was bringing me to his clan—pack members he claimed were my people—so I didn't want to burden him with the fact that a creature was on the hunt for me.

At least, not until I had a chance to meet my family. To discover who I really was.

"You certainly are. I don't know how you managed to survive so many years in the human world."

I looked at him as a thought surfaced. "Why were you in the human world if it's such a dangerous place?"

A strange expression crossed his face as he gazed at me sideways. It was gone a second later.

"I loved adventure. Still do, though it's no longer in the cards for me. The human world, while dangerous today, has a lot of our history to reclaim. Many years ago, long before we were born, the human world welcomed shifters. Clans would even exchange goods with them."

"Really?" I didn't know much about the relationship between the human world and shifter ones, so this information more than intrigued me. "I need to learn more about our history."

"You will, though I don't think you should ever enter the human world again."

I cocked an eyebrow, but before I had a chance to ask him why, he continued.

"I'm assuming your wolf surfaced under the Fallen Moon?"

I nodded.

"Yeah, I can sense her, and she's so much stronger than when we first met." He raked his fingers through his dirty blond hair and sighed. "I think if you entered the human world again, she'd take over, and you wouldn't be able to control the shift. Your wolf would feel protective and want to surface. But shifting in the human world is dangerous."

I had so much to learn about the two realms I was connected to—the human world where I was raised and the Silver Creek realm where I was born. Right then, I made a pact with myself that once I'd figured out a way to survive the shadow creatures that were bound to come for me, I would spend time learning all I could.

Until then, survival was the name of the game, and it was the only thing I could think about. I prayed Silver Creek would offer me some protection.

Dawson pulled a small satchel from his pocket and peered behind us as if checking to see how far we'd gone from Thunder Cove. Then he bent down and sprinkled what looked like salt onto the ground—it was the second time he'd done that—but before I could ask him about it, he pointed to a narrow path in the forest just ahead.

"The portal to Silver Creek isn't far from here. We're almost home."

My weary feet were relieved to hear it, but the rest of me bristled in fear at the thought of entering a new realm.

Home.

The word sounded so foreign to me. All my life, I hadn't felt at home anywhere. I assumed it came with the territory of being an orphan. Though in the last few days, my heart was forced to acknowledge I'd always longed for that special place where I fit in, where I belonged.

But would that be Silver Creek?

Dawson seemed to sense my concern.

"This is your clan. There's no doubt you're one of us." He nudged me with his elbow, and a ghost of a smile crossed his lips. "It feels good to be bringing you home."

"How can you be so sure they'll accept me?"

"You'll have to trust me," he murmured, his voice low and insistent. "You have nothing to worry about."

I wanted to believe him, but as I peered at him from the corner of my eye, I wasn't so sure he believed what he was saying. He looked troubled, as if he too was working through his thoughts.

"Right around the corner."

The men and wolves who'd been trailing behind suddenly closed the distance as a strange arc of blue light appeared up ahead, its bright fingers stretching out on the ground as if to guide us.

Above the light was a deep carving of what looked like a wolf. I recognized the Silver Creek symbol with it.

"There's the portal."

Dawson glanced over his shoulder. His men seemed to understand his silent command and stayed close behind us.

"You've passed through a portal before to get into this world," he said as he reached for my hand. "But hold on tight. I don't want to lose you."

"Lose me?"

But before he could explain, we were swallowed up by the dazzling streaks of color that swirled around, cloaking us in its brilliance. I took a deep breath and held his hand tightly as fear traced its spiny fingers down my back.

"Dawson?"

I didn't hear a response, but his hand tightened around mine as I took another step forward.

Passing through the portal felt strange yet inviting, like a hot summer's breeze washing over my face, but a few steps later, vibrant hues of pink and silver bloomed in front of my vision as a world, far brighter than anything I'd ever seen, came into view. While the sun had been setting in Thunder Cove, it shone high and bright in the sky at Silver Creek.

Panic tightened my chest at the realization I'd somehow let go of Dawson's hand. I spun on my heels, trying to stare back through the portal, but there was no sign of him or his men—only the same blinding light.

I crossed my arms over my chest, unsure what to do.

Should I follow the path ahead or wait for Dawson and his men to appear?

Before I had time to decide, I heard footsteps and let out a breath when Dawson appeared in front of me.

"I told you not to let go." He chuckled, but the smile quickly vanished from his lips.

I watched in confusion as he looked around in search of something, his mouth drawn into a scowl.

"What is it, Dawson?"

The sounds of his men stepping through the portal were all I could hear, but Dawson remained tense. A tingle of fear licked up my spine, and I shivered when I saw his eyes had darkened.

"This way," he said, ignoring my question, though he reached for my hand again. "Let's get you home. I'm sure you're exhausted."

As we made our way along a perfectly manicured trail with its smooth stones flanked by massive trees and flowers of all colors in full bloom, my mind trailed back to the day at the carnival when I'd been overtaken by a vision so vivid it had left me spellbound.

The vision had revealed a path just like the one before me, leading up to a magnificent castle. And as I walked along, with Dawson by my side and his men trailing close behind, my thoughts were once again a tangled mess, though one thought refused to be ignored.

I was headed toward my clan, my family, and my future.

There was no going back. I'd finally get answers and discover who I truly was.

And I should've been beyond thrilled.

But as a castle came more fully into view, complete with a dark stone gargoyle whose watchful eyes stared down at me as if warning me I shouldn't be there, I couldn't help but wonder if I'd made the worst mistake of my life.

CHAPTER TWO

DAWSON

Seeing Ember again caused my heart to pound so loudly in my ears, I could barely hear her voice over the thrum of its thunder.

But now that she was safely in my realm, I could relax. Sure, there were a ton of questions about her parents and why they'd left her in the human world. But I already had men busy investigating, and I was sure they'd come back with answers soon enough.

As for the clan, I'd told Ember the truth; they were excited to meet her.

Well, *most* of them, anyway.

My mother had been oddly quiet when I told her I was headed to Thunder Cove to bring Ember home. She'd glared at me with daggers in her eyes, though I made sure my tone brooked no argument.

Richard, my father's former beta, was the one who'd adamantly tried to convince me that bringing a stranger into our clan was nothing short of irresponsible. It wasn't the first time since I'd become Alpha that he'd tried to interfere with my decisions.

I respected the man. He'd been by his Alpha's side for years, but my father was no longer here to lead the clan—that was unfortunately now my job—and Richard needed to accept that.

Besides, somehow, I knew Ember posed no threat. She belonged at Silver Creek.

But as we made our way along the path toward home, all I could think about was the bitter taste that had hit the back of my throat.

Dark magic.

It had been brought into my realm, and I needed to find out why.

I turned to Ember. Her blue eyes were wide as she took in her surroundings. I would've laughed at the childlike expression on her face if I wasn't so distracted by the sense of danger on the horizon.

"Thank you." I nodded to Craig, whose job had been to make sure we'd made it back through the portal safely. "I knew I could rely on you, as always."

When I'd left for Thunder Cove, I wasn't sure what to expect or whether Rylen had told Craig the truth when he'd promised that he'd help Ember reach the meeting spot just outside the Thunder Cove territory in a neutral zone. When I'd seen that he'd kept his word, I was more than a little surprised. The Thunder Cove's beta was anything but trustworthy.

Craig shot Ember a bright smile and extended his hand. "It was a pleasure to meet you. Welcome home."

One thing I could count on, other than steadfast loyalty, was that Craig would always be kind to anyone he felt needed it. From the way Ember worried her bottom lip, it was clear she was more than a little nervous about being here. Still, she reached out and slid her hand into Craig's, who shook it gently before stepping away.

"Thanks," Ember whispered. "I appreciate that."

Craig's gaze settled on me once more, apparently wanting to

double-check that I no longer needed him. Then he and my men headed off into the city for what, I assumed, would be their usual night of drinking and gambling.

"Is that your castle?" Ember pointed off in the distance to the cream-colored spires that appeared against a crystal, blue sky.

"No, that one belongs to my mother," I replied. "Mine is a bit further ahead."

"It's beautiful." She took a tentative step forward and then picked up her pace as we strolled along the trail leading to the center of town. "I haven't seen a castle before."

"Well, you'll more than see one. You'll be living in one."

When she peered at me, a look of confusion crossing her face, I chuckled.

"I had a room set up for you in court. It's where all the royals live."

"Royals? But I'm not—"

"It doesn't matter. And besides, we don't know that yet. But until we do, I want you to stay close. It's in your best interest."

As soon as the words came out of my mouth, I realized how ominous they sounded.

"Our realm is quite large, so until you've gotten familiar with the land, I think it's best you stay close to the central court, that's all. You'll find everything you need there, and I'll never be far. Don't be afraid to come to me if you ever need to."

"You're the Alpha."

It wasn't a question.

"Yes. My father passed away not too long ago, and I was the next in line. Being an only child didn't leave me with much choice."

"I'm sorry to hear about your dad," Ember replied, her voice gentle. "You said you weren't left with a choice. Does that mean you didn't want to lead your clan?"

I took a deep breath as memories of my father's passing flooded my mind.

In the final moments of his life, he'd confessed his sins, and in turn, he'd broken my heart. I'd always held my father in the highest regard—I'd worshipped him—but once I knew what he'd been capable of, my hero had been reduced to a desperate man, too hungry for power to see beyond it.

And now, I carried the burden of the shame that came with safeguarding his secret. I felt like an imposter, as though I had no right to be Alpha.

Still, he'd meant a great deal to me in life, and that didn't change in death. I wouldn't betray his legacy no matter how much the truth haunted me.

"It isn't the path I would've chosen for myself, no, but it is what it is. I'll do the best I can to fill some rather big shoes."

"You all seem so young to have so much responsibility," Ember replied thoughtfully. "The Alphas of Thunder Cove and Cody..." She paused as though it pained her to speak about them, but then she cleared her throat and continued, "I was beyond impressed by how well they take care of their clan."

"Were the Alphas of Thunder Cove kind to you?" My chest tightened at the thought of Grayson or Alex mistreating her. It had been years since I'd been able to call them friends, and while I'd once known them to be gentle, good-hearted men, time and power could undoubtedly change a man.

"Oh, they were wonderful," she said quickly, and I couldn't help but notice how her voice softened, filled with emotion. "It was hard to leave them, but after I shifted under the Fallen Moon, my wolf needed to meet our clan, and I knew we wouldn't find that in Thunder Cove."

I bit the inside of my cheek as a streak of jealousy cradled my heart in a possessive grip. She felt something beyond simple gratitude toward the men who'd helped her, but that was none of my concern. My role, as Alpha, was to ensure her safety and reunite her with our clan. Other than that, I had no claim to make.

"So, you don't have any idea who my parents are?"

I wasn't surprised by the question, only that she hadn't asked it sooner. Throughout our journey to the portal, she'd been deathly silent. I felt she was someone who thought carefully before she spoke and only asked questions she already knew the answers to.

"Not yet," I replied honestly, as my gaze swept over her hopeful expression. "But we'll find them. It may just take some time." I paused, not wanting to dampen her spirits. "You have to understand that it would be difficult for a member of the clan to come forward and confess to leaving their child in the human world."

I swallowed the lump forming in my throat at the thought of a she-wolf being left to fend for herself in such a hateful realm. "Shifters don't abandon their young. I'm sorry that happened to you."

"I survived," she said calmly. "Besides, it's not important to me. My wolf wants to know her clan. But my parents, whoever they are, they're not my family. Maybe I can find my place in your clan despite them."

I was more than a little caught off guard by her words, and as much as I heard the pain in her voice, I also sensed her strength. She'd fortified her heart against the idea of ever meeting her parents, but now that the possibility was real, perhaps she wasn't sure she was ready for it.

"That one." I pointed to the castle only a short distance away, flanked by two smaller versions. "That's Castle Alastair. My home—*our* home. We're almost there."

I could tell she had many more questions to ask by the way her eyes kept flashing over to me, but she only nodded and continued moving, keeping up with my pace.

"You'll be in the eastern wing. There will be people to look out for you, take care of anything you need. I have some business to attend to in the Great Hall, so that'll give you time to rest for a few hours."

She nodded again, but this time her eyes never met mine. Instead, she peered around as though she wanted to commit the cherry blossoms and glacial-blue sky above to memory. It reminded me of how lucky I was to live in such a wondrous place. It was too easy to forget when I'd grown accustomed to such beauty.

I walked Ember through a side entrance of the castle, hoping to avoid the crowds I knew would be gathering in anticipation of meeting her. She needed time to relax before she was faced with hundreds of shifters who'd have questions for our newest member.

"When will I meet the clan?" she asked as though reading my mind.

We moved through one hallway after the next, each lined with large paintings of our past Alphas. Ember took it all in, her head twisting from side to side as if she didn't want to miss a thing.

I paused, as I always seemed to lately, by the illuminated portrait of the Alpha before my father. It was a habit I needed to break, yet for the life of me, I couldn't seem to walk by without feeling drawn to it.

Then we strode up the grand staircase and down the final hallway which would lead to her room. But as we drew nearer, the scent of dark magic returned to me. I sputtered at the taste of it. It was as though it had followed us into the castle, its venom leeching onto my skin.

"Dawson? Are you okay?"

"Huh? Oh," I stammered, realizing I'd left her question unanswered. "You'll meet my family this evening at dinner. And then I'll introduce you to the rest of the clan tomorrow night if that sounds good to you."

"That sounds wonderful." She cleared her throat, and for a

moment, I wondered if she could taste the darkness as well, but I dared not ask. "I'm looking forward to meeting everyone."

Her lips curved into a smile that never quite reached her eyes, and I felt a deep sadness. I'd tried my best to reassure her everything would be okay, but I knew my words were simply that, words. And I got the feeling she'd been promised many things throughout her life which had never come true.

"And here we are." I opened the set of double doors, leading to the eastern wing, their silver trim sparkling in the bright light from the large windows. "This is all yours. Go explore, and I'll see you soon."

I reached out, not wanting to overstep or make her feel uncomfortable, but still wanting to comfort her however I could. To my surprise, she seemed to welcome my touch, and when she took a tentative step forward, I banded my arms around her.

"I know you've been through a lot, but you're home now," I whispered into her hair. "This is where you belong. With us. You're going to be happy here…and safe."

She nestled her head against my chest, her fingers running over the triangle crest on my cloak—a silver tree and pink leaves that wove their way around each branch—the symbol of the Silver Creek clan.

"I promise, Ember."

Her name was nothing more than a whisper, a sacred vow on my lips.

I finally let her go, and when she stepped back, her expression had somewhat changed. Gone was the look of apprehension and uncertainty. Instead, her eyes gleamed with what looked like steadfast optimism, and it nearly took my breath away.

She was certainly a Silver Creek she-wolf. There was no mistake about that. I couldn't wait to see her in her true form.

As I watched her walk away, my heart soared with over-whelming relief that she was finally where she belonged.

I'd promised her she'd be safe and happy here. When she glanced back at me and smiled before disappearing around the corner, I knew I'd go to the ends of the Earth to make sure I kept my promise.

And it started with uncovering who was responsible for bringing darkness to our doorstep.

CHAPTER THREE

CODY

When I woke up, my body thrummed with the need to have Ember again, but when I reached out, she wasn't there. I wiped the sleep from my eyes as my surroundings came into view.

Alex was still sound asleep on the other side of the bed, but Grayson was gone, likely preparing for the upcoming meeting with the Silver Creek clan.

Quietly, I crawled out of bed, not wanting to wake Alex, and made my way over to Grayson's closet to snag a t-shirt and a pair of pants.

"Hey, have you seen Ember?"

I turned to see Grayson standing in the doorway, a stack of papers in his hand.

"No," I replied. "I figured she was in her room."

He shook his head. "She wasn't here when I got up. I asked Liza, but she hasn't seen her either. Maybe she went for a walk or something." He nodded toward a pile of white shirts with the Thunder Cove crest stitched into the shoulder. "Put on one of those. I'm going to call a meeting this morning about Silver Creek. I've decided to cancel."

I cocked an eyebrow. "What made you change your mind?"

He took a deep breath, then let it slowly escape his lips. "Because it'll only raise questions we aren't prepared to answer. You were in the human world, same as them. It's best we leave it be. At least for now."

I was relieved he'd decided to let it go. I didn't want to have to explain to members of Silver Creek why I'd been in the human world. I was also worried about how Grayson might react when faced with seeing members of their pack, especially their Alpha. The last time they were in the same room together it didn't end well.

I pulled one of the shirts from the stack and slipped it over my head, then smoothed my fingers over the ocean-blue insignia of our clan. "I'm going to go look for Ember," I said as he handed me a pair of pants that would be at least a size too big, but they'd have to do until I could get back to my place. "What time is the meeting?"

"In a couple of hours. I'm going to wake Alex to give him time to shower and eat," he replied. "Hey, when you see Ember, tell her there's a package waiting for her in her room."

"A package?"

Grayson scowled, clearly annoyed at my questioning him. "Yes, a package. Just let her know."

He left the room while I finished getting dressed. I was more than a little curious, so I made my way into Ember's room at the end of the hall. Sure enough, sitting on the bed was a large box, wrapped in red wrapping paper, complete with a huge bow.

Whatever was inside would be left a mystery until I found Ember, but from the look of it, Grayson had suddenly gotten in touch with his softer side. He'd changed so much in such a short time, all for the woman with the blue eyes and curves that I ached to feel in my hands. The thought made me growl with desire as I headed downstairs and out into the busy streets in search of Ember.

It wasn't long before I ran into Selena, who, to my surprise, rather than having her arms loaded with shopping bags, was carrying a stack of books. "I haven't seen her," Selena told me when I'd asked about Ember. "Did her wolf surface last night? I tried to look for her, but I couldn't find her." Her gaze was downcast, and she blushed. "Then I got distracted and—"

"Yeah, her wolf surfaced, and she was gorgeous." I grabbed a few of the books from Selena's arms before they fell to the ground. "But when I woke up this morning, Ember wasn't there. I don't know where she could be."

Selena smiled, a knowing look on her face, and I realized that I'd just given away the fact that I'd spent the night with Ember. But there was no time for idle chatter, and I wasn't interested in explaining anything. As we rounded the corner leading to her house, I picked up the pace.

"I'm worried, Selena."

She pursed her lips. "Why? She probably woke up and wanted to shift again. I mean, her wolf has been waiting a long time for this."

"I know, but she can't just go off on her own without letting us know. It's too dangerous, especially since she's only shifted once. Once she's gotten used to it, she can explore on her own, but until then—"

"Cody, she'll be fine. Give her a bit of breathing room." Selena set her pile of books down on the front step as she unlocked her door. "She's just letting her wolf live a little." She cocked an eyebrow. "You should try it once in a while yourself."

I sighed, handing her the books I'd been carrying once she had the door open. "I'm not trying to be controlling. I need to make sure she's okay."

The truth was, I was concerned about something other than Ember shifting by herself. What I'd discovered in the pages of the ancient text hadn't left my mind since I woke up to find she was missing. *What if a creature from the shadow realm had taken Ember?* I'd never forgive myself for not protecting her.

I also couldn't pick up her scent anywhere, which bothered me.

How was it possible that she could've left without a trace?

"Cody, I understand how you're feeling, but I'm sure she's not far." Selena rested her hand on my shoulder. "You're worrying over nothing."

"Nothing?" I lashed out. "I brought her into our world, so it's my job to look out for her." I couldn't control the frustration in my tone, even though I knew I was taking my anger out on the wrong person. "She can't venture off on her own so soon. Not yet. Not without me. What if she accidentally wanders into a portal?"

Selena furrowed her brow at my words, her eyes suddenly downcast. It was clear she finally understood the risk of Ember heading off on her own.

"I'll keep an eye out for her, and if I see her, I'll tell her you're looking for her."

"Thanks, Selena." My shoulders sagged with worry, but I tried to shake the heavy feeling as I made my way across town and headed toward the forest. If Ember had awakened to the power of her wolf begging to be free, chances were, she would've run out of the city and into the great outdoors.

I wouldn't stop looking until I found her.

"Hey!" I spotted Rylen off in the distance and started in his direction. Despite how many times I called out to him, he didn't seem to hear me. "Rylen! Have you seen Ember?"

Finally, he turned around as I closed the distance.

"I can't find her anywhere."

"No, I haven't." Rylen cleared his throat and nodded to the path which led into the forest. "Maybe she went for a run. After the Fallen Moon, I'm seeing a lot of clan members in their true forms. It'd probably be best if you let Grayson and Alex know. I think they'll need to call a meeting to remind everyone of the rules."

I shook my head. "We expected the power of the Fallen Moon would have that effect on them. Our Alphas aren't going to want to enforce anything just yet. We'll give it a few days for the power to fade, and then I'm sure everything will return to normal."

"If you say so," he replied gruffly. "I hope the power never fades. I haven't felt stronger in my entire life." Rylen stretched his neck and then rolled his shoulders as though he might shift at any moment.

"What happened to your shoulder?"

His eyes darted down to what looked like deep scratch marks. Five red streaks lanced across his skin.

"Tree branches. I couldn't stop myself from running through the forest last night. It must have been hours before my body finally gave out. It felt so fucking good."

I nodded as the memory of racing with Ember under the light of the Fallen Moon surfaced. She'd been so beautiful in her true form, a powerful she-wolf with a bluish-gray coat that shimmered in the moonlight. I'd never seen anything so stunning.

"If you see Ember, please ask her to return home. Tell her I'm looking for her."

Rylen practically snarled at me, but before I could ask him what his problem was, his expression softened, and he shrugged.

"Sure, if I see her, I'll let her know." He turned and went in the opposite direction but then stopped and looked back at me. "We should focus on helping Grayson and Alex lead the clan. There's a lot to be done, alliances to form, decisions to make. They're going to need our help."

I stared at him, puzzled by his words. Of course, we'd help our Alphas with their responsibilities as we always had.

"Ember has been nothing but a distraction since you brought

her here. Grayson isn't the same, and Alex has had his head in the clouds for days." His eyes narrowed, filled with accusation. "And you..."

"I what?" I stepped forward, daring him to accuse me of neglecting my duties. I'd been nothing but loyal to my Alphas; I'd take a silver bullet for them. I wasn't going to stand there and allow Rylen to insinuate otherwise.

"She isn't one of us. I'm surprised the clan didn't revolt when they discovered that you guys had brought her into our realm."

His tone held an edge as sharp as a fae's blade, and with it, his words sliced across my heart. I wanted everyone to accept Ember for the powerful she-wolf she was. The realization that my fellow beta was apparently against her more than angered me.

"Tread lightly," I warned him as I took another step forward, my fists clenched as rage roared through my body. "Who are you to question the decisions our Alphas make? You're a beta. It's your job to stand alongside them, no matter what."

"No matter what?" Rylen clenched his jaw, and it was clear that he, too, was struggling to control himself. "Above all else, I'm loyal to the *clan*. That's who I work so hard for. Not the passing desires of its leaders."

"Being loyal to the clan means being loyal to our Alphas. Don't question them again, or it'll be the last time you do."

I expected him to retreat, to realize that come what may, our allegiance to Grayson and Alex superseded our own wants and needs. Whether he agreed with Ember being part of our clan or not didn't matter. Just like her not being my mate didn't matter. If she chose to love only Grayson or Alex instead, I'd stand by them. It was more than a simple vow I'd taken when they honored me with the role of beta; it was my calling. My clan meant everything to me, and so did the two men who'd been there for me since we were kids.

But Rylen stood firm, and any hope that he'd realize how traitorous he sounded quickly vanished when he chuckled darkly and rolled his eyes.

"Leaders come and go, Cody. You know this as well as I do. What matters is that we always look out for the clan, first and foremost. Hopefully, one day soon, you'll come to understand that."

Before I could respond, he dropped to his knees and shifted into his true form. His wolf, as black as midnight, seemed to have grown impossibly larger since the Fallen Moon, and it left me speechless.

He snarled at me, then darted away, his hind legs kicking up dirt as he tore across the field. I watched in amazement at how quickly he moved, his beast gracefully crossing the miles as though he was flying.

And then he was gone.

Ember.

As my thoughts returned to her, I let the change take over. Gray fur, streaked with flecks of white, began to sprout from my forearms, then my muscles grew tense as they stretched and thickened.

My senses were much sharper as a wolf, and right now, I needed all the help I could get. As soon as my wolf emerged, I took off running. Before my mind could register where I was headed, I found myself in the middle of a wheat field that edged our property.

Then I caught it. It was faint, but I'd know the scent anywhere.

Ember.

My legs moved as quickly as they could, my determination to find her intensifying as I headed in the direction where her scent was the strongest, my nose following it like a beacon calling a lost ship home to shore.

And that was what I felt like with Ember, not in my arms. As though I was navigating dark waters on my own. I needed her with me, as close as possible, to fill the hollow ache which was left behind when she wasn't near.

Her scent grew stronger as I made my way north. My heart galloped at the thought of being reunited with her—of being able to pounce on her, play with her, and love her with everything I had to give.

The night before, when we'd made love, it had been blinding in its intensity, but it was only just the beginning of our lives together. I didn't know what a life with her would look like exactly or how we'd make it work, but I didn't care. A life without her wasn't an option.

"My Alphas and my woman."

I picked up speed, racing through the shadows of the forest, the shade from the canopy above doing nothing to cool the scorching flame of desire that burned within.

"Ember! Stay where you are! I'm coming!"

As I bounded in the direction of her intoxicating scent, which led me beyond our territory and toward the Silver Creek portal, my heart sank when her smell suddenly disappeared without a trace. I frantically darted across the field in an attempt to pick it back up, but it was gone.

"Ember!"

There was no response. Wherever she was, she was likely too far away to hear my cry. As I spun around, my nose trying desperately to pick up the trail, I felt powerless.

I continued searching for what felt like hours, following endless paths that led in circles, always returning me to where I started, no farther ahead.

I finally collapsed to the soft ground when my wolf could endure no more, and as my body sunk into a crumpled heap, so did my heart.

But I wouldn't give up. Even if it took me the rest of my days, I wouldn't rest until I had Ember back in my arms where she belonged. My mate or not, I didn't care. I couldn't—wouldn't—stop looking for her.

"Ember!"

CHAPTER FOUR

EMBER

It's okay to miss them, but we're where we need to be. Now, they'll be safe.

Cody. Grayson. Alex.

My wolf's voice had grown louder in the last few hours, and as my thoughts ran rampant, I welcomed her reassuring presence.

We were one being, but two *very* different personalities. My wolf was fierce, steadfast, and fearless, while I was a quivering mess of uncertainty and confusion, constantly second-guessing myself.

As I explored the castle and took in the beautifully decorated rooms and the history entrenched on the walls and behind glass cases, all I could think about were the three men who'd saved me and brought me into their world.

But not everyone had been happy about that.

I shivered as I recalled what Rylen had said to me as he'd tackled me to the ground. He'd told me the clan wanted me gone and that half-breeds like me were nothing more than parasites who should be destroyed.

Leaving was the right thing to do. Even if Rylen had been

lying to me and the clan would've accepted me since I'd finally shifted, I was a liability, a problem that Grayson, Alex, and Cody shouldn't have to worry about.

They'd done more than enough for me.

But as I strolled alone through the hallways of the majestic castle, wondering what the future would bring, I didn't want to think about experiencing any of it without them.

Those strong and passionate men had made me feel things. Things I was too afraid and too stubborn to accept.

As I rounded the corner of another long corridor, I found myself entering what appeared like a hall of sorts, and I realized it was probably the Great Hall Dawson had mentioned earlier, though he was nowhere to be found.

A large, painted crest dominated the far wall, set between two floor-length pink and silver stained glass windows. Farther back, there was a large platform, highlighted by its decorative stonework, while several gray stone pillars supported the impressively high ceiling.

I stood in stunned silence for a few moments, taking in the expanse of the room. It was clear this place was of great importance to the clan. I could almost envision a group of trumpeters blasting out from an upper gallery as the royals entered.

I took a step forward, ambling between two large tables in the center of the glossy, marble floor, streaked with flecks of pink and silver.

The Silver Creek clan indeed stayed true to their brand.

I continued making my way across the room, where a series of large portraits hung proudly in gleaming, silver frames, high-lighted by dim overhead lights.

I couldn't help but imagine myself in a real-life fairytale. That was how it felt as I drank in the beauty around me.

But this wasn't a fantasy, and I wasn't a princess. Though, with the silly decisions I'd been making lately, I *could* probably qualify for the role of court jester.

"Ember, right?"

I turned toward the voice and came face to face with a petite woman, though she looked anything but fragile. Her auburn hair fell in glossy waves down to her waist, and it complemented her wide, green eyes which were tipped up at the corners, but it was her outfit that piqued my curiosity.

She was dressed in black leather pants, and her abs were highlighted by a tightly fitted t-shirt. Her look was completed with a pair of shit-kickers.

She looked like a total badass.

"Yeah, that's right. Nice to meet you." I extended my hand, but she only glanced down at it and smirked.

"You're not at all what I expected. Thank God for that."

I shrank beneath her intense gaze but managed to keep eye contact.

When she was done studying me, she nodded toward a small door off to the right, one I hadn't noticed before.

"Did you meet her yet?"

"Huh?" I eyed the door, unsure who she was talking about. "Who?"

"Ciara. She's a total monster. Pure evil. She doesn't want you here, so keep your distance. Take it from me, she's not an enemy you want to have."

She eyed the door again as if she was waiting for it to burst open at any minute. Then she refocused on me, her stare even more intense than before. "Don't trust her. If you do, it'll be your funeral."

"I don't understand," I replied shakily as a shiver of apprehension trickled down my spine, its icy fingers crawling across my skin.

"I have to go, but I'll see you later." She turned away and headed toward the corridor but paused. "Just be careful."

"Wait!"

But before I could ask her who Ciara was, the stranger was

gone, leaving me standing in the middle of the Great Hall, wondering what the hell had just happened.

∾

"You look rested." Dawson's steel-gray eyes were on the darker side but carried a lively spark as he came into the room.

Dawson had told me dinners with his family were always formal, but I wasn't expecting him to show up in a tuxedo. He looked regal as I supposed all royals did, but there was a laid-back vibe about him, which made me think if it were up to him, he'd be wearing a t-shirt and jeans rather than the suit.

"I've been taking it easy," I replied. "I was exhausted, but I'm feeling a lot better now."

It was the truth, though my insides still quivered from my earlier conversation with the redhead in the Great Hall. Since then, I'd stayed in my room, fearful I'd run into this Ciara person or perhaps others who didn't want me here. I wanted to ask Dawson about it, but for some reason, I hesitated.

"This tie is driving me crazy."

Dawson walked further into my room in search of a mirror. When he found one, he readjusted the tie of his black suit while I stood there, unable to take my eyes off him.

He was a cross between sinfully handsome and boyishly charming, and though he hadn't exactly made me swoon when we first met, he certainly was now.

"If you're a royal, shouldn't you be wearing a crown and a cape?"

An effortless grin broke out on his face, and it was one of the sexist things I'd ever seen. "We do wear crowns, yes, but only at special ceremonies. But capes, no. We leave those for the superheroes."

I studied his expression for a moment before realizing he

was teasing me. His eyes danced, acknowledging the cheesiness of his joke.

"When you came to Thunder Cove, you and your men looked like you'd walked straight out of a cosplay event."

"Cosplay?" he asked. His breath exhaled on a half-laugh. "I'm not sure what that is, but we only wear our surcoats when we're on official business."

"And coming to get me was official business?"

He shrugged, all smiles. "The *most* important official business."

I rolled my eyes, though his answer tripped up my heartbeat.

"I really am happy you look rested." He offered me his arm, much like he had when he came to Thunder Cove for me. "But you also look beautiful."

He'd sent someone to my room earlier to ask for my sizes, and then just like with Cody, I'd soon found a closet filled to the brim with clothing.

It was all so surreal, having people buy me things, but I was grateful to be looked after, and when an older woman had shown up with another parcel in hand which included a soft pink dress and diamond-encrusted, silver heels—my attire for the evening—I'd thanked her profusely.

She hadn't uttered a single word to me, but her smile had been warm, as was the gentle hug she'd given me before leaving the room.

My face grew hot, but I held his gaze. "Thank you," I replied, smoothing down the pink dress. "And you look like a million bucks."

"Is that all?" he teased, his attention anchored on me. "Maybe I need to up my game."

I laughed as he escorted me down the stairs and through yet another series of hallways. The castle felt endless, and I knew with my misguided sense of direction, had I wandered too far earlier, I'd likely have never found my way back.

"You're going to meet my mother, my father's only sister, and Richard. He's been around since I was a kid, so he's like family. He was my father's beta."

I couldn't help but notice how Dawson seemed almost pained to mention the man, and I wondered what the real history was between them.

"Do you have dinner every night with your family?" I asked.

The idea of sitting down and sharing a meal with people I loved was something I used to long for, especially at Thanksgiving and Christmas. All the television sitcoms I used to watch as a kid had depicted families passing platters of food around and rooms filled with laughter.

"God, no," he replied raggedly. "I couldn't handle it more than once a month."

I cocked an eyebrow, and he chuckled deeply. "They're not *that* bad, don't worry. But my aunt tends to drink a little too much wine and then pokes her nose into my personal business, especially my love life. And my mother is always finding something to complain about."

When he noticed I'd grown quiet, he squeezed his hand around mine, the one that had been clutching his arm for dear life.

"My cousin will be joining us as well. She could care less what my mother thinks, and I admire that, especially since it drives the old bags crazy."

He laughed again, and despite my nerves, I couldn't help but smile. "I think you'll like her."

We rounded one final corner, and as we entered the room, my jaw dropped. It was even nicer than the hall I'd discovered earlier. Glittering chandeliers draped in jewels hung over a long, elegantly decorated table filled with white candles and trailing flowers.

Martha Stewart, eat your heart out.

I took a deep breath and hoped I wouldn't stick my foot into my mouth or do something foolish. I wasn't great at first impressions, and suddenly, it felt imperative that Dawson's family liked me.

After all, these were important members of what was now *my* clan.

"Take a deep breath," Dawson whispered to me, and I was beyond thankful he let me hang on to his arm for just a few more minutes. "They're going to love you."

I didn't need them to love me, I only needed them to accept me. As Dawson pulled out my seat, nodding to me that it was going to be just fine, I smiled to let him know I appreciated him. Then, I straightened my shoulders and tried to look as dignified as possible, though I felt more than a little out of place.

"Cousin, why the hell do we put ourselves through such torture every month? I feel like you need to remind me again."

I looked up to see a face I barely recognized making her way into the room. Gone was the outfit straight out of an action movie. Instead, she wore a stunning emerald-green dress and matching heels. Her long, red hair had been artfully twisted into a crown of ringlets, with tiny flowers placed inside each curl. Even her freckles were barely visible beneath her perfect makeup.

She patted Dawson on the shoulder, who chuckled and gave her a quick hug.

"You're the Alpha now. Can't you just put a stop to these painful events disguised as so-called family dinners?"

"You know how much they meant to my father," Dawson replied. Then his lips curved into a smirk as he recited something he'd obviously heard a thousand times before. "Family dinners are what keeps—"

"Yeah, yeah," the redhead sighed. "Us connected. Well, maybe I don't want to be connected to these fools."

Dawson laughed. "This is why I'm glad you're here. You keep things interesting."

The woman smirked, but it was clear she was happy to see Dawson. "You're lucky I love you, cousin."

"Jasmine, meet Ember," Dawson said, turning to me.

"We've already met," Jasmine replied, her green eyes sliding over to glance at me before taking a seat. "She was wandering around the Great Hall earlier. And since I was sure you hadn't prepared her, I warned her about Ciara."

Dawson opened his mouth to say something, but before he could, movement behind us caught our attention as two women entered with a tall, broad-shouldered man trailing closely behind.

"Good evening," the woman in the front said, her steely gaze flickering over Jasmine before resting on me. At that moment, the very air in the room seemed to change, as though the woman's presence made it hard to breathe.

"Speak of the devil, and she shall appear," Jasmine mumbled before filling her wine glass and downing it in a few gulps.

Then, whatever was hovering in the air faded, and I took a deep breath, thankful to have my lungs back. I peeked around, but no one else seemed to have been affected.

The woman's lips, painted a blood-red, offered me a forced smile, as a man—apparently a butler—entered the room and pulled out a chair for her, but she waved her bejeweled fingers dismissively before sitting down, and he scurried away.

"Well, aren't you going to introduce us, Dawson?"

"Of course," Dawson replied. "This is Ember, the newest member of the Silver Creek clan."

He reached under the table and squeezed my leg, which I hadn't realized was jittering so hard I was nearly rocking in my chair. His touch helped to steady me, and I steeled myself for the rest of his introduction.

"Ember, this is Richard. I told you earlier, he was my father's beta and has been a loyal member of our family for most of his life."

"*All* of my life," Richard firmly corrected him. He tipped his head to me before taking a seat between the two women.

He was a fierce-looking man with deep lines etched into his weathered face and darkness in his expression that looked almost haunted.

"And this," Dawson continued, nodding at a woman with long, red hair who I knew must be Jasmine's mother, "is Beatrice, my lovely aunt who can't seem to stop meddling in my affairs."

The woman scoffed. "If only you'd listen to your elders. You seem to have inherited my brother's predilection for tuning me out."

Lovely certainly seemed like an odd way to describe a woman whose features appeared to be trained into a permanent scowl, though despite that, I could sense a glimmer of warmth underneath her tough facade.

I swallowed down the discomfort I felt and smiled as Dawson extended a hand toward the woman at the head of the table—a woman who hadn't taken her eyes off me since she'd entered the room.

"And this is my mother, Ciara."

Ciara.

Her cruel gaze lingered on me for another moment before she whispered something to Richard, who chuckled darkly.

"Mother," Dawson growled, clearly irritated by her rude behavior. "Ember is now a member of Silver Creek, and I expect everyone to show her a warm welcome."

When his mother didn't so much as blink, he peered over at Jasmine, whose lips curved into a knowing smirk, which told me she knew *exactly* where the conversation was headed, though I was clearly out of the loop.

"Jasmine, I feel a celebration is in order, don't you?" Dawson smiled fully then, the expression causing playful sparks in his eyes. "It'll be the perfect way for Ember to meet the entire clan all at once. It should be a grand event. A night the clan will always remember."

"Absolutely, cousin," Jasmine replied. She narrowed her gaze on Ciara, who looked horrified. "An event suitable for a *queen*."

Ciara's reaction was one of a wounded animal, and for the first time since she'd walked into the room, her expression lost a bit of its sharp edge. This time when she looked at me, her eyes held a challenging gleam I didn't quite understand.

"It's a pleasure to meet you, Ember," she murmured, her finely arched brows drawing together slightly. It was clear she'd rather douse me in gasoline and light a match than speak to me. "I trust you're settling in well."

"I am, thank you."

"Dawson, I'd like to hear your thoughts on forming an alliance with Sable Crest," Richard said, and I was relieved to no longer be the focus of conversation.

"Oh, Richard," Beatrice groaned, a frown on her face. "How many times have we asked you not to talk about clan affairs at dinner? You can hold a private meeting with Dawson for those discussions. We just want to enjoy a nice meal." She winked at me, and it brought a smile to my lips. "And perhaps lots of wine."

"Besides, you shouldn't speak about clan matters in front of total strangers." Ciara scowled, clearly directing her comment at me. The tilt of her head as she studied me with narrow, cold eyes emphasized she wouldn't be easily convinced I deserved a place at the table, much less the clan.

"Or in front of people who have no say in the matter," Jasmine added, her words as sharp as a dagger. "I'm sure Ciara doesn't want to be bored by such things which don't concern her."

If looks could kill, Jasmine would've been dead on the floor next to me.

"I care about all matters relating to *my* clan," Ciara bit back, her eyes growing impossibly wide as though she was shocked Jasmine would dare insult her. "I'm the Alpha's mother." She peered at Dawson out of the corner of her eye. "He should consult me as his father did."

Beatrice flinched, and I got the impression she'd had to manage many hostile conversations between her daughter and sister-in-law over the years. "What's on the menu for this evening?" she asked, trying to steer the conversation to a lighter topic. "I'm famished."

As if perfectly timed, a group of women entered the room, their arms filled with platters of food. I was thankful for the interruption and even more relieved when Ciara busied herself with Beatrice and Richard, appearing to have lost interest in me.

I thanked the woman who set an assortment of appetizers in front of me while Jasmine leaned toward me, a satisfied smile plastered across her pretty face.

"I warned you, she's pure evil," she whispered, as though we were old friends in cahoots together. Then she waggled her eyebrows dramatically in an apparent attempt to make me laugh. "A total monster. But I have a feeling you can handle her."

She lifted her wine glass from the table and gave me a playful jab in the ribs with her elbow.

"Welcome to Silver Creek, Ember. Cheers."

CHAPTER FIVE

DAWSON

I'm so sorry.

The words floated through my mind aimlessly as I walked Ember back to her room after dinner. I wanted to tell her how sorry I was for the way my mother had treated her.

She'd just arrived; I should've let her enjoy a quiet evening exploring the grounds rather than a stuffy dinner affair with a woman who'd viewed her as though she was nothing more than an intruder.

"Hey," I said, pausing at the split in the corridor. One hallway led up to her wing, the other out through the back courtyard. "Would you like to take a walk with me?"

"I'd love that."

I took her hand, winding my fingers through hers as though we were long-lost lovers.

If I was honest with myself, from the time I'd felt that strange connection at the carnival, I hadn't been able to think about anything else but her. But I wasn't going to push myself on her. Holding her hand was enough for me, and I was thankful she let me.

I led her through the back gate and out into the gardens. The path below our feet shone differently at night than it did during the day. Now the grounds were limned in silver. The cobblestone sidewalks glowed against the dark expanses of lush, green grass, and the trees bore silver leaves against their inky trunks.

"Your realm is breathtaking," she murmured, soaking in the dazzling lights and flower beds draped in the moonlight. "Have you always lived here?"

"I have," I told her. "Wolves don't usually move away from their clans. It's a dangerous world for us out there."

We strolled toward a path to our right, the one that led to the portal, but then I veered away from it and guided her in the opposite direction.

"Not everyone wants peace. I'm sad to say. Most realms are at war with one another."

"Cody told me about that...the dangers of other realms," she replied. "I guess where I come from is no different. Countries are always fighting with each other, just the same."

She took a deep breath as though the thought of warfare pained her. "The more I think about the human world, the happier I am to be away from it. It feels like I'd lived a life in shades of gray. But now..."

"Now...what?" I stopped, turning to study her when she grew silent.

Finally, the corners of her lips cracked into a smile, though the moonlight gave her away, and I saw tears glistening in her eyes.

"I know it sounds cheesy, but now I feel like I'm living in color."

I wanted to tug her into my arms and tell her everything my heart demanded of me, but I knew it would be selfish. She was just happy to be with her clan and to have found a place that felt like home.

The memory of how terrible my mother had treated her resurfaced, sending a blaze of fury down my spine.

"I'm sorry."

She stared at me in confusion, and when she opened her mouth, I shook my head to silence her.

"I'm sorry my family didn't welcome you as I expected they would."

"Oh," she replied, shrugging it off for a moment before her expression turned to one of raw emotion. "I understand, Dawson. Your mom doesn't know me. I'm a stranger who appeared from out of nowhere."

She reached out and rested her hand on my arm as if she wanted to drive the point home. "You're lucky to have a mom who's so protective of you. Of your clan."

Ember was giving her far too much credit, but as I gazed down at her under the moonlight, any thought of telling her that my mother would likely never accept her vanished.

There were only two words I needed to say at that moment.

"*Our* clan." I gazed into her eyes, hoping she could see how much I believed in that, how much I meant it.

"I like the sound of that." Her voice was light, whimsical. "I'm excited to meet everyone tomorrow."

She stepped back. A playful grin danced across her lips. "I mean, after meeting your mother, I feel like I can handle anything."

I laughed and wrapped my arm around her shoulders as we traveled away from the more developed area.

There were still definitive paths, but they were composed of tamped earth instead of cobblestone. The trees were thicker and fuller out here. The grass grew longer. It was quiet except for the soft rustle of the wind through the leaves.

Ember gasped in awe as tiny fireflies made stunning light shows over the surrounding fields.

When I tipped my head back, I saw that the stars were brilliant—thousands and thousands of them, brighter than any diamonds I'd ever seen. It was as though the heavens wanted to embrace Ember and show her she truly was home.

"Look," I murmured as we crested a hill and gazed down into a valley. The center of the meadow was bathed in a shimmering light, but it wasn't what I wanted to show her.

The creatures below, who'd stamped out a circle in the grass to bed down for the night, were creating their own illumination of silvery light, which sparkled as they moved.

Long, spiraling horns protruded from their foreheads and emitted a luminescence that outshone the moon above. Their hides were sleek and pure white, and despite the fact we were a distance away, they were easy to see.

"Oh my God," Ember breathed. "Unicorns."

A smile tugged at my lips as I caught the gleam of the excitement in her expression.

Several adults mingled in the circle of trampled grass, brushing their cheeks against each other and swinging their silky tails affectionately. The young ones, tiny versions of their parents with stubby horns, frolicked in and out of the circle but never strayed far.

"They aren't usually found in realms where wolves like us live," I told her as she stood in stunned silence. "But we've always welcomed them. I think we're the only shifter realm who does."

She shook her head slowly in bewilderment but never took her eyes off them. "They're magnificent," she whispered.

I wanted to tell her the unicorns weren't the only glorious creatures bathed in moonlight, but I couldn't seem to find the courage, nor did I want to ruin the moment. There were so many things I wanted to show her, so many adventures I wish we could experience together. But I was painfully aware that my responsibilities as Alpha had to come first.

"I've only ever read about unicorns in fantasy books," she

said, her gaze transfixed on the scene below. "I'm so happy to know they're real."

I cocked an eyebrow. "Fantasy books, huh? When I was younger, if I wasn't on an adventure of my own, I always had my nose stuck in one of those. My friends used to tease me relentlessly, but I didn't care."

She turned to me, her smile bright. "I'd only read about worlds like this. And here you were, living in one." She nudged me playfully. "And I'm glad you didn't listen to your friends. Girls love guys who are bookworms."

I laughed. "Well, that's good to know."

"Thank you for this." Her hand slid around my back, her fingers tensing against my skin. "And for bringing me into your realm. I've never felt so at home anywhere in my life. I can't explain it..."

Her voice trailed off, but it was fine with me. I didn't need an explanation. I couldn't imagine spending a lifetime away in a different realm, never knowing my family.

And at that instant, I found the bravery to take a leap of faith and follow my heart, no matter how little I knew of her. It had once led me across some carnival grounds to where this curvy beauty stood. And however it had happened, it had led me here —to this moment—with her.

I leaned forward, my eyes locked with hers, pausing for just a second. Then my arms banded around Ember possessively, gradually tightening as I brought her to my chest, just as I had earlier.

"You're all I can think about." I stared down at her when she lifted her face to mine, our bodies pressed together.

My heart was like an engine roaring inside me, every cylinder firing. There was no going back now. I knew it was a lot at once; she'd only just gotten here, but time seemed irrelevant. I felt connected to her as though we'd known each other our whole lives.

"Ever since we met, every waking thought has been about you. I was worried sick...I tried everything to find you. I even returned to the human world, but you were gone."

I hated how my voice cracked, but I couldn't seem to hide my desire, not with her in my arms and the truth on my lips.

"Dawson," she replied with a sigh, never breaking eye contact. "I have to tell you something, and you're not going to like it."

I leveled her with a frank gaze. "Nothing you tell me will change how I feel."

She opened her mouth in protest, but I kissed her softly, silencing her words. I meant for our kiss to be gentle, short. But somehow once my lips were on hers, I couldn't seem to stop. One kiss turned into two and three. It was a long series of unending kisses, one leading into another, my tongue claiming hers possessively.

"The way I feel about you...this connection...I just can't ignore it," I whispered when I broke the kiss.

She breathed a sigh against my mouth. "But, Dawson, you don't know me."

Her eyes turned downcast as though she was hiding a secret that would somehow change my feelings for her, but I ran my fingers under her chin and lifted her face. I needed her to look into my eyes and see what I'd told her was the truth.

It didn't matter where she came from or what scars she hid behind her gorgeous smile. We may not have spent much time together, but she was wrong. I *did* know her. I knew her soul. Her spirit. Her fire. And my wolf growled at the thought of meeting hers.

I gently swept the hair away from the nape of her neck and sprinkled kisses down her soft skin. "I know what I feel," I whispered. "I don't need to know more than that."

I lost track of time as we stood beneath the stars, the moonlight shining above us, my mouth on hers, my kiss a promise of what was to come if she wanted it, if she was ready to give me a chance.

She gave back equally, her lips and tongue meeting mine in a dance of fire until I finally took a step back, knowing my desire was verging on reckless. Ember's eyes danced in the faint light as she gazed up at me. One corner of her mouth curved into a smile, so knowing it felt as if she were staring right through my skin and into my heart.

She wasn't ready to let go or for the night to end. Not yet. Not under the light of a perfect moon.

I closed the distance between our lips, pulling her closer, weaving my fingers through her hair. My lips found hers again, crushing and passionate, our kiss searing this time, more intense than our last.

Every one of my senses was alive. Each touch of her fingers on my skin left a trail of fire, fanning the flames of deep longing I had for this woman.

When we were breathless, our legs threatening to give out on us, we sank to the grass, my arm wrapped around her, just watching the scene below. And for the first time since I became Alpha, my body relaxed. This woman, a stranger to my life, but not my heart, gave me strength and courage I didn't know I had.

And she did it without trying, just by being near.

A rush of power, like the dominant surge of the ocean, pulsed inside my chest, rising and falling, as I thought about how happy we could be together, with her ruling by my side. I never wanted the moment to end.

But I knew the hill we sat on wouldn't be the only one I'd have to climb if I wanted to claim her heart. The way her eyes burned bright whenever she spoke about Grayson, Alex, and Cody told me more than words ever could.

She had real feelings for them. Feelings that may never fade.

I pulled her into my arms, and we tilted our faces toward the sky, our eyes glued to the ocean of stars as though the heavens above held all the answers.

As we watched, one flew across the sky, a comet with a bright tail streaking behind it. Before it disappeared, I closed my eyes and made a wish.

A wish for Ember to be mine, a wish for a future together.

CHAPTER SIX

GRAYSON

My mind raced as I tried to understand exactly what Cody was telling me. All this talk about how there were *two* types of lupus interfectorems—hunters who claimed souls and shadow beasts who guarded them—had set my teeth on edge.

I peered over at Alex, who sat silently at his desk, deep in thought. I needed them to explain this to me before I tore the roof off the meeting hall.

"So, these hunters could've possibly entered our realm to claim Ember, and you never fucking told us? Now that her wolf has surfaced, she's in even more danger."

I glared at Cody, who stared me down as though he had nothing to be sorry for. Yet he did. He should've been on his knees begging for forgiveness instead of challenging my authority with an unapologetic gleam in his eyes. An expression I wanted to knock off his face.

He had no right to keep that information to himself.

"If I'd told you, you would've forced her to leave," he replied pointedly. "And I wasn't about to let that happen. She needed us, our protection."

"This guy," I growled as I paced the room, "didn't think for a minute his Alphas should know that a goddamn shadow creature could've attacked our clan at any moment." I closed the distance, my fist ready to smash into Cody's face. "You couldn't have saved her on your own. You aren't a fucking—"

"I'm not a what, Grayson? Tell me, what am I not?" Cody sprang to his feet, and while I would've thought he knew better than to get in my face, he didn't hesitate. "I'm a beta and not an Alpha? What else? Your family created the clan, and mine didn't? I know." He practically snarled his words. "We *all* know because you don't stop reminding us every chance you fucking get. So, what do you think I'm not that I haven't already heard a hundred times?"

"You aren't a fucking *hero*," I said. "No matter how hard you want her to be your mate, she isn't yours. That's what you told us, right? That she was no one's to claim. Yet you put our clan's safety on the line for her."

"And I'd do it again."

"Stop." Alex raked his fingers through his hair and puffed out a breath. "Cody was wrong in not telling us."

"You're fucking right; he was wrong!"

"But so were we," Alex continued. "We brought Ember into our realm. That's on us. We knew she'd been attacked by a wolf slayer which we knew very little about and what it could mean. We're the ones who decided to put our clan in jeopardy. Not Ember."

"Now she's gone, and we need to find her," Cody added.

We need to find her.

Rage had consumed me since Cody had shown up at our doorstep, looking disheveled and more than a little frantic, with the news that Ember was gone.

"What the hell do we do?" I asked them, despite knowing they had no answer. "She could be anywhere."

Cody sat next to me, but I refused to make eye contact. I was still furious with him. Angry he'd withheld such vital information from his Alphas. Outraged he'd taken it upon himself to decide what was best for the clan.

And above all else, livid he hadn't brought Ember back home.

"We'll find her, Grayson." Cody's tone had weakened, as though he'd burned through every ounce of his energy searching for Ember. When I finally turned to face him, I could see it in his eyes. He had. He hadn't stopped looking for her until his body had given out.

I was still fuming, but I knew staying mad wouldn't bring Ember back. We needed to band together if we stood any chance at finding her.

But if we didn't bring her back soon, there'd be hell to pay.

"You picked up Ember's scent, and then it disappeared." I stood and faced Cody, who looked as though he'd suddenly gotten a second wind. "What's the closest portal to where you lost track of her?"

Cody's gaze clicked over to Alex as though he was trying to decide whether to tell me or not. The look could only mean one thing.

"Silver Creek." Just saying the name of the clan left a bad taste in my mouth, and my rage suddenly returned with a vengeance. The thought of Ember being in that realm with a man who'd betrayed me made every muscle in my body grow tense.

Cody nodded and then stood up next to me. "But why would she leave for Silver Creek?" He scrubbed his face with the palm of his hand. "None of this makes sense."

"Ember's wolf just surfaced," Alex replied calmly. "We have to trust she had her reasons for leaving. And you know we can't just storm into Silver Creek looking for her," he cautioned, knowing full well it wouldn't matter to me. "It could cause a war."

How he was still sitting at his desk, looking as though everything would be just fine more than pissed me off. But that was Alex. Always calm, always thinking things through. It's what made him a great Alpha. But now wasn't the time for that laid-back energy. I wanted him to be as fired up as Cody and I were.

"A war?" I pressed my lips together to keep from snapping back, but it was useless. "Why the fuck would Silver Creek start a war over us going there to get Ember? You're not making any sense."

"They would if she belongs to their clan," he replied, vocalizing what I already knew, but didn't want to hear. "The night of the Fallen Moon reveals many things, Grayson. Mates, friendships, power... It isn't hard to believe it revealed to her who her clan was."

It took every bit of control I had not to lunge at him and shut him up, but it was Cody who spoke up next, and his words shocked me. I expected him, of all people, to be willing to go to the ends of the world to bring her back, no matter where she was.

"He's right, Grayson. If we go into Silver Creek's realm, trying to bring her back, her clan could revolt against us, even if she tells them she wants to leave. They're just as protective over their pack as we are."

Ember couldn't belong to Silver Creek. She was too kind, too good. And even if she'd been born there, it didn't mean that was where she belonged. Besides, she didn't know what was best. How could she? She'd only recently shifted. Her wolf would be longing for adventure without understanding the dangers of exploring other realms alone.

"We also have to consider she may not want to be brought back," Alex added. "She might be better off there, especially if they're her clan."

"You know what, Alex?" I asked, ice running through my veins at how calm he appeared. "You're fucking dead inside. Do you ever feel passionate about anyone? Anything?" I spun, ready to storm out of the room and take matters into my own hands. I'd had enough sitting around.

"Just because I don't shout at the top of my lungs or lose control doesn't mean I don't care, Grayson. Because I do."

"You have a funny way of showing it," I bit back, turning my head toward them but keeping one foot out the door. "Ember deserves a man who'll be there for her, no matter what. And anyone who truly cares about her *should* be shouting at the top of their lungs and losing control right now because she could be in real danger."

Alex took a deep breath, and for a moment, I wondered what it would take to push him over the edge. In all our years of friendship, I'd only ever seen him lose his shit once, and that was when Jackson had disappeared. But if he cared for Ember, he wouldn't be able to sit still like he was.

"You can fire at me as you always do, Grayson. But it doesn't change the truth about how I feel."

"And what truth is that, Alex?" I took another step out the door. I wasn't in the mood to hear him explain himself or try to calm me down with his smooth words. I wasn't about to wait around for something to happen. I had to get out and look for Ember, even if it meant violating clan law and entering Silver Creek without permission.

"I'm in love with her, Grayson."

I stopped in my tracks, but I didn't turn around to face him. I couldn't. Because I knew he'd see through me if I did.

It was the first time I'd ever heard Alex say those words about anyone. And as much as I'd been raging about how casual he'd appeared to be, once he'd said those words, I wanted him to take them back.

Because even though I didn't always understand myself or why I did some of the things I did, I knew one thing in my heart of hearts.

One thing I couldn't deny, even to myself.

It was one thing to spend an evening sharing Ember with Cody and Alex. That was raw desire, intensified by the light of the Fallen Moon, or maybe just lust. But when I'd awoken in the middle of the night, unable to sleep, with Ember curled up next to me, I knew what was responsible for my sleepless night.

I was in love with her too.

I only hoped it wasn't too late. That if Ember was at Silver Creek, she wouldn't want to stay—that she wouldn't be seduced by their wealth, their position.

And above all else, I hoped one day I'd have the chance to tell her how much she meant to me.

CHAPTER SEVEN

JASMINE

I had to admit, I liked Ember. From the moment I'd found her wandering the Great Hall the night before, I knew she was someone I wanted to get to know. Her vibe was refreshing and genuine, unlike so many of the pretentious women I'd spent most of my life around, with hearts as hollow as a rotting oak tree.

And an added bonus, Ember being around could take the heat off me for a while and perhaps distract my horrible Aunt Ciara, who'd been pressuring my mother to set me up with a member of the Sable Crest clan—a mate I *didn't* want.

I knew the only reason Ciara even cared about my love life was because she hoped I'd fall in love with a member of another pack and leave my own. I was nothing but a nuisance to her, especially after my uncle had died and I'd stopped giving a damn about what she thought. When I was a kid, I was terrified of her—we all were—especially after hearing rumors of her banishing members, or worse. But I wasn't afraid of her anymore. I refused to be. But I was worried for Ember. While Silver Creek was an honorable clan, there was no way Ciara would ever accept Ember into the pack. Not just because Ember was a halfling—something Ciara despised—but because it was evident from the way Dawson looked at Ember, there wasn't anything he wouldn't do to make her happy.

And it was clear as day, that outright pissed Ciara off.

The bitch was used to being the matriarch of the family who played by her own rules. As much I didn't want to harp on Dawson about how he needed to get out from under her thumb now that he was Alpha, I wished he'd cut her down a notch or ten. She wasn't a good person, much less someone he should trust.

And if the midnight whispers I'd heard countless times outside the Great Hall after our family dinners meant anything, she was also having an affair with Richard and probably had been for years.

It was one of the many secrets I was sure she carried around with her, except I was also certain *everyone* knew.

Everyone but Dawson.

Then again, he hadn't been around much the last few years, always off exploring one realm or another. It was only since he'd become Alpha that he'd stayed close.

If only his father hadn't gotten sick with an illness which took him so quickly. One day he was holding a clan meeting, the next he was confined to a bed, too weak to even stand. At least when Dawson's father had been in good health, he could control Ciara.

I wiped a tear away at the memory of his passing. I knew Dawson never wanted to be Alpha, and my heart had broken for him when he found himself forced into the role. He wasn't born to lead, though I'd never say that out loud. Dawson was like me, someone who wanted to be free to explore, to follow our hearts and find adventure around every bend.

"Your mother is going to be a problem for Ember," I told Dawson as we strolled through the garden.

He'd asked me to meet him, which was unusual. He rarely

took time out of his busy schedule for such things, which was why I attended those annoying family dinners every month. It was the only time I got to see him.

"I can handle her, and so can Ember," he countered, though it was clear he'd been struggling with how brash his mother had been with Ember the night before. "Though my father would be so disappointed in her for the way she's acting. It's not Ember's fault she was taken from this realm and left in the human one. I'd expected my mother to show a bit of empathy."

"Sorry, dude, but this is your mother we're talking about. She's an elitist who thinks she's better than anyone else, especially a halfling."

"It makes me sick to my stomach. Ember deserves so much more after all she's been through." Dawson eyed me thoughtfully as he plucked a rose from a nearby bush. "Flowers. Music. Dancing. I want tonight's celebration to be everything she could dream of."

I didn't have the heart to tell him a party was like putting a bandage on a bullet wound. While a celebration welcoming Ember into the clan was a wonderful idea, it wasn't going to fix the main problem—getting Ciara under control so she didn't cause problems for Ember.

"And your mother?" I asked him, hoping he might realize just how savage his mother could be. "What do we do about her? She'll ruin the evening if we let her."

"Then we won't let her," he replied before handing me the rose. "My mother needs to learn a lesson in humility, and who better to teach her than a girl who wants nothing more from us than to be accepted?"

"You've gotta be kidding," I snorted, shaking my head. "How do you expect Ember to teach your mother a lesson in anything?" My usual cool tone was displaced by anger at the thought of how cruel his mother could be. I'd had my fair share of encounters where Ciara had me feeling as though I was worthless, that I'd never amount to anything. I didn't want Ember to be her next victim. "If it were up to her, she would've banished me years ago."

"You know I'd never let that happen, so I don't know why you'd say that." Dawson looked away, his eyes distant and slightly hard for a moment. "My mother doesn't make decisions for my realm. That's my job."

A thick silence descended between us, and I couldn't stand it. Things should be easy between us like they used to be, yet something was bothering me—something I couldn't shake free from my mind.

"You need to start showing your mother you aren't a pushover." I didn't mean for it to, but it sounded more than a little snarky.

"She knows her place," Dawson replied, and I could tell I'd annoyed him. "And if she doesn't, she soon will."

"I'm sorry, I never meant to—"

In public, I addressed him as Alpha and wouldn't dare challenge anything he said. But in private, we were cousins, childhood friends, and I hoped he appreciated that I'd always be honest with him.

Dawson waved off my apology. "You have nothing to apologize for, Jasmine. Come on."

He walked with me toward the back of the gardens, then through the large gates, which led to an all-too-familiar path. I raised my eyebrows when he turned and headed in the direction of the portal.

"Dawson? Where are we going?"

His expression clouded over, and he took a deep breath but kept walking. "I sensed something when Ember and I made our way through the portal yesterday."

"What do you mean, you sensed something?"

"Something dark."

His words hung in the air between us.

"Dark magic?" My eyes darted around as I tried to pick up on anything out of the ordinary. "Who would use dark magic in this realm? It doesn't make sense."

"I know." Dawson squared his shoulders, his expression grave. "So, why can I taste it? Smell it? It's as though it followed me home."

"Do you think it has something to do with Ember?" I caught my breath and stiffened at my own question

"No," he replied firmly. "It's not possible."

The emotion in his voice left me troubled. I didn't sense that Ember possessed any sort of magic, but what if we were wrong?

"I need to shift."

Without hesitation, Dawson's shirt ripped as he dropped to his knees, and I watched while his wolf appeared. When we were kids, we'd laughed about how easy it was to fool people because our wolves looked so much alike. But years later, his wolf had grown to twice the size of mine, though our unusual gray and silver coloring was still the same.

I followed suit, closing my eyes and tilting my head back to allow the sun to wash over my face as the transformation began. The stretch of every muscle felt so wonderful as my body contorted and primal power rushed through my veins.

Though some of us could sense dark magic easily, I'd always struggled to smell or taste anything outside of the call of the forest, the bark of the trees, and the fish in the lakes. Still, as I stood there on all fours next to Dawson, I finally caught a whiff of what he'd sensed.

It was faint, like a rotting garden, off in the distance, filled with corpse flowers, but there was no denying it had been there.

What are you going to do, Dawson? Should you alert the clan to be on guard?

Dawson pawed at the ground as if the source of dark magic had burrowed itself into the earth, and he wanted to pull it out by its roots.

"Here," he replied. *"It's here, beneath our feet, right at the entrance to the portal."*

I peered at him curiously as he unearthed what looked like a small, silver coin. I took a step closer as he dug a little deeper around it and realized it was a ring.

"What is that?"

He studied it closely, easing to his forearms and then flipping it over with his paw as though he recognized it somehow.

Then I watched, my heart dropping, as his head lowered to the ground in despair. His energy changed, and I sensed him losing control as rage roared through his body.

"Dawson?"

He tilted his face to the heavens, and the growl that escaped his lips was like thunder as the ground rumbled beneath my feet. I took a step back in confusion.

"What's wrong? What's going on?"

He didn't respond, but when he lowered his head, his gray eyes burned in rage, and it sent a streak of panic across my underbelly.

I'd only ever seen that look on his face once before, back when we were much younger. He'd ventured off as he always did, with one of his closest friends at his side, only to return home days later with this same haunted look in his eyes.

He'd refused to talk about what had happened, but it had somehow changed him, hardened him. It had only been since he'd brought Ember here that I'd begun to see the old Dawson return, the man who wore his heart on his sleeve.

He took off running, his paws barely touching the ground, his movements propelled by pure rage. Whoever was responsible for having brought dark magic into our realm was about to answer to an enraged Alpha with murder in his eyes.

CHAPTER EIGHT

DAWSON

I got dressed as quickly as I could, my fingers barely able to manage the buttons of my shirt as my mind raced with how I was going to deal with such treachery.

The source of dark magic had been brought into my realm by one of our own, welcomed by someone I trusted.

I heard her voice before I saw her, her tone nearly a screech as she scolded one of her housekeepers, who went rushing off. The moment I rounded the corner and she saw me, she froze. It was clear she knew what I was there for.

"How dare you?" I clenched my jaw as rage rippled through my body. "I knew you had a witch use magic to call me home, but this…" I lifted the silver ring, and she recoiled as though she'd been stung by a hundred bees. "This reeks of *dark* magic."

Rather than deny what she'd done, my mother pursed her lips and scoffed.

"You were gone too often and too long." She stared up at the portrait of my father hanging above the fireplace. "I told your father he had to do something about it, but he refused. He was always too soft on you, so as always, I had to take matters into my own hands."

"But why dark magic? That was your solution for keeping tabs on me? To force me back whenever you wanted?" I knew my mother could be selfish, but I would've never imagined she'd welcome dark magic into our realm simply so she could control me.

"Dark magic," she replied, her lips curving into a smirk. "Isn't *all* magic dark? That's what everyone in this realm thinks, isn't it?" She waved her hand in the air as though she couldn't be bothered to explain herself. "I paid a witch to spell your signet ring. It allowed her to bring you back whenever I needed you here."

I drew in a sharp breath, my anger threatening to boil over, but before I could say another word, my mother walked over to the mantle and lifted the lid of a small box and pulled something from its depths.

"Here," she continued, offering me what appeared to be some sort of relic.

I stared down at her palm, unsure what I was looking at. It was as dark as coal and oval-shaped, no more threatening than a pebble, yet I knew better.

"It was a simple enchantment spell, Dawson. I'd invite the witch here whenever I needed you. She'd hold this in her hand, say a few words, and then you were brought home. There was nothing more to it."

I stood rooted in place, refusing to touch the object. She finally closed her hand around it and placed it back into its box.

"You had no business welcoming a witch into your home, much less into our territory. You know how dangerous they can be."

I'd calmed down a little, but I was still furious. The truth was, as much as I had despised my mother forcing me to come back to this world when I was on one of my adventures, if she hadn't used the services of a witch to summon me home that final time, I would've never had a chance to say goodbye to my father.

I took another deep breath, letting the air slowly escape my lips. "The witch is never to step foot in this realm again. Is that clear?"

My mother flashed me a smile that told me she'd quickly agree but only because she no longer had use for a witch. She knew I couldn't easily chase after my thirst for adventure now that I was Alpha.

"*Crystal* clear, Dawson."

I spun on my heel, but before I left the room, I tossed my ring into the roaring fireplace, hoping the flames would destroy whatever remnants of magic flowed through it. I watched as purple smoke briefly appeared in a puff before disappearing.

"I mean it, Mother," I warned her. "If you ever bring magic into my realm again, I will banish you." I nodded toward the burning ring. "And then you can spend the rest of your life with your witch…in *her* realm."

My mother firmed her chin, but it was apparent my words had affected her. Ciara Alastair thought herself a powerful she-wolf, but even she wouldn't survive in a world of covens.

As I made my way out of the room, I thought about how Ember would be meeting our clan tonight and Jasmine's warning that my mother might ruin the event.

"One more thing," I added before leaving her to lick her wounds. "I expect you to treat Ember with respect. She's part of this clan, and whether you like it or not, she isn't going anywhere."

"You talk to me about bringing magic into this realm, yet you welcomed the likes of her." My mother had found her fire again, nearly spitting out the words. "You don't know what you've done, Dawson. That girl is trouble."

"That *girl*," I growled, "is here to stay. Make me choose, Mother. I dare you. Because if you create problems for her, I will." I turned to her, wanting her to know, with certainty, just how serious I was. "And you won't like the outcome."

"And you, my son," she hissed, her almond-shaped eyes blazing with anger, "will not like the outcome of having brought that girl into our realm. She doesn't belong here."

I left my mother standing in the center of the room, with that wild expression on her face, but as I rounded the corner leading to the front door, I couldn't deny the knot in my chest as her threatening words seeped into my spine.

The way she'd stared at me was as though she held all the power, and I was nothing more than a child she could manipulate. It was a dangerous look which bordered on lethal.

I made my way home, the knot in my chest growing with every step. I'd seen my mother furious before, yet this had felt different somehow. I couldn't shake the sense there was more to her antics than I was understanding.

That somehow, if I didn't keep a close eye on her, she might pose a threat even greater than bringing dark magic into my realm.

CHAPTER NINE

EMBER

"I'm nervous as hell," I blurted out as Dawson led me into the Great Hall. The room buzzed with energy and voices, though they grew silent when I appeared. "I hope I don't make a fool of myself. Or of you."

Dawson walked proudly next to me, a grin plastered on his face which told me he wasn't at all worried I'd say the wrong thing or do something to cause chaos amongst the pack.

I only wished I had his confidence.

"They can't take their eyes off you," Dawson reassured me. "Everyone is so excited to meet you."

I blew out a sigh of relief as we made our way between the lines of people who greeted us with smiling, curious faces.

"Welcome home, Ember!" one woman squealed as another waved at me from the growing crowd.

My pulse raced as excitement quickly replaced the fear that had previously taken up residence in my chest like an unwanted squatter.

But as I walked deeper into the crowd, I couldn't help but wonder whether my parents were here, too afraid to claim me, to admit what they'd done.

My heart sank at the thought, but I tried my best to push it away. Tonight was about meeting my clan, and I wanted to enjoy every moment. I refused to let my anger at my parents take that away from me. They'd already stolen so much.

As we approached the head table, a young girl ran up to me, her hands full of posies.

"These are for you!"

My heart did a flip-flop as I accepted her precious gift, and she beamed at me before her mother appeared at my side, apologizing.

"This is all she's been talking about all day," she told me. "It's been a very long time since we welcomed a new member to the clan."

"I'm thrilled to be here," I replied as she shooed her daughter away.

Another child, a boy this time, ran up to Dawson and revealed something in the palm of his hand.

"Ahh," Dawson said with a smile that could melt a glacier. "Wolf glass!"

"Wolf glass?" I asked, peeking at the smooth, red stone in the boy's hand. "It's so pretty."

"Wolf glass is only found after a Fallen Moon," the boy added proudly. "So it's very rare."

"Then you must be a very special boy to have found it," I answered, and his grin grew even bigger.

We took our seats at the head table, and I couldn't help but notice several empty chairs to the right and left of us.

Dawson had mentioned it would be a grand celebration, but he hadn't filled me in on any other details. I was just grateful to be able to meet the clan all at once, but as I saw his mother enter the room, surrounded by Richard, Beatrice, and some others I hadn't yet met, I was filled with apprehension.

"Ember, I'd like you to meet Anita, Gia, and Maria," Dawson murmured, and when I turned my head, I saw a group of women standing next to our table. "They've been asking to meet you all day."

The three women appeared to be around my age, and each of them gave me a warm, genuine smile. The girl in the middle, Gia, looked like she wanted to ask me something but was too afraid to speak up.

"It's nice to meet you," I told them as they came closer to me when Dawson got caught up in conversation with Craig, who appeared to be in great spirits.

"And it's so nice to meet *you*." Anita looked at the other girls, and then her gaze returned to me. "We haven't met a halfling before."

"Anita! What the hell?" Gia scolded her. The look on her face told me she was fearful her friend had insulted me.

I laughed. "It's okay. That's exactly what I am. Though, to be honest, since my wolf surfaced, I'm starting to forget what it felt like to just be human."

"We've never been to the human world," Anita continued. "What's it like?"

"Well…" I began as I thought about how I was the wrong person to ask such a question. My life hadn't exactly been a good one in the human world. But when their questioning expressions begged for an answer, I told them about how I'd worked at a carnival and how we even shared a lot of the same things as the shifter realms, though it suddenly dawned on me I hadn't seen a car since I'd entered this realm.

"Do you drive?"

"Oh, no," Maria exclaimed as though my question was an outrageous one. "Our realm doesn't have automobiles or anything like that."

When I cocked an eyebrow in surprise, Anita laughed.

"Our Alphas wanted to keep things simple here, so we just have horses, but…" She leaned in closely, obviously not wanting everyone to hear what she was about to say. "We're hoping

Dawson will change things. Other realms have all the technology, but here, it can get a little boring."

"Anita, that's not true," Gia replied, her eyebrows narrowing, and I got the sense she was the serious one in their trio. "Our realm is beautiful. Special. And if we try to be like the other shifter realms, we'll lose that."

"If you say so." Anita rolled her eyes. "I'm just saying it would be nice if we had some of the modern things other realms have. We're lucky we even have electricity."

"You're so dramatic sometimes," Gia countered.

I smiled. "Your realm is such a wonderful place, and I agree, it's very special."

Dawson reached out for me, his hand resting on mine. It was clear he'd heard what I'd said. The women giggled as though they were surprised to see such affection from their Alpha, and then they wandered off. Another man appeared next to Dawson, and he was once again swept up in conversation.

It was evident from how people lined up to speak to Dawson, he was an Alpha they respected. I thought about how he'd told me that he hadn't been their leader for very long, but from the look of it, he was doing a fine job.

"I see you have your own fan club."

I turned to find Jasmine, who looked just as beautiful as she had the night before. Dressed in a deep blue dress and matching sandals, she easily caught glances from the men who watched us from afar.

"I don't know about that." I laughed. "But I appreciate how friendly everyone has been. By the way, you look amazing."

She took the seat next to me and immediately opened a bottle of wine.

"You're looking pretty good yourself," she replied, handing me a glass. "How are you holding up?"

Before I could answer, Ciara suddenly appeared before us. Her lips were in a straight line, and it was clear she was deep in thought. But then there was a slight lift to her lips which could almost pass as a smile.

"This is *your* night, Ember," she said, awkwardly pointing one long finger at me. "I hope it's everything you've dreamed of."

Her words caught me off guard, and I scrambled with how to answer. The night before, she'd been so cold and distant with me that I wasn't expecting such a quick change of heart. But I was beyond grateful for it.

"Thank you so much, Ciara." I glanced around the room as even more people filed in, hoping to meet me and speak with Dawson. "I'm so happy to be with my clan. I feel at home here."

And it was true. Despite how terribly I missed Grayson, Alex, and Cody, being in Silver Creek somehow made me believe that come what may, I'd be okay. I didn't feel safe exactly —how could I with a beast from the shadow realm after me— but at least I could breathe.

Still, I knew I had to tell Dawson I was marked. I'd tried to tell him last night, but we'd been swept up in the moment, and I'd lost my chance.

I took a deep breath as the guilt from letting Dawson kiss me —and kissing him back—resurfaced, just as it had many times since last night. But I couldn't deny the way he made me feel.

It was so easy to be around him. I felt comfortable, like I could be myself.

"I'm happy to hear that," Ciara replied, and I blushed, thankful she couldn't read my thoughts. "That's the power of being with your people. Wolves are naturally strongest amongst their pack. *Humans* don't seem to have the same type of connection to one another."

I didn't miss the way she'd said the word, and it was clear she still thought of me as mainly human, though she kept her tight-lipped smile plastered on her face. I couldn't blame her for being cautious of me. After all, I was a stranger to this clan, to her. It would take time, and that was okay with me.

"My wolf has never been more at ease," I told her.

My words seemed to please her, and despite Jasmine trying to get my attention in an apparent attempt to shoo Ciara away, she didn't seem to notice.

"I have something for you." She handed me a black, velvet case which seemed to come from out of nowhere. "It's a special gift for an extraordinary occasion."

"Oh, you didn't have to do that," I stammered. I'd never been good at accepting gifts, and for obvious reasons, this whole situation felt exceptionally awkward. It was clear Ciara didn't like me, so this was the last thing I was expecting.

"Go on, open it," she insisted.

I lifted the lid.

"Oh my God," I gasped, nearly at a loss for words. "Oh, Ciara. It's beautiful."

"Holy shit," Jasmine mumbled, obviously impressed by the pink diamond necklace glittering up at us. The pendant was huge, larger than any diamond I'd ever seen.

I ran my fingers over the sparkling chain, woven in delicate strands that knotted around itself. It was smooth to the touch, and it took my breath away.

"I don't know what to say," I sputtered. "Thank you so much."

Ciara cleared her throat as though my gratitude made her uncomfortable, and when I looked over to Jasmine, she wore an expression that was more than a little suspicious.

"Suddenly, you're so generous," she said to Ciara. "I don't think I've ever known you to give such lavish gifts."

Ciara's mouth formed a large O, making it clear she was severely offended. "Ember has been away from her clan for a long time. This is my way of welcoming her home." Her gaze latched on to the diamond necklace that rested in my fingers. "Aren't you going to put it on?"

"Yes, of course. Thank you." I fumbled with the chain, my trembling fingers struggling to undo the clasp.

Dawson finally turned his attention to us, and his jaw nearly dropped.

"This is gorgeous." The look on his face was equal parts relief and shock. "It's perfect for you." He reached over and gently pulled the necklace from my fingers while I turned. I made sure to keep my hair low to cover the mark as I allowed him to fasten it around my neck.

When I turned back to face Ciara, she nodded approvingly. "It looks wonderful on you. I'm glad you like it."

"Oh, I love it." There were no words for how appreciative I was, how much this gift meant to me. "I'll cherish it for always. Thank you."

"You're welcome," she said before her gaze clicked over to Dawson. "Richard would like to speak to you whenever you have a moment. He'll be escorting me tomorrow on my way out of town."

"Where are you going?" Dawson asked her.

She sighed as though revealing her plans to Dawson made her weary. "I'm going to see my cousin at the Sable Crest clan. I'll only be there for a couple of days."

"And you cleared it with their Alpha?"

"Of course," Ciara replied as though Dawson's question was a ridiculous one. "But you know better than that. I don't need any more approval to enter their realm than they do ours. It's only Thunder Cove who enforces such nonsensical rules."

My ears perked up at the mention of Thunder Cove, and it was clear Ciara noticed. She peered at me curiously as if to gauge whether my loyalty was to them or Silver Creek.

"Wouldn't you agree, Ember? That such a rule is outrageous amongst wolf packs? We should be able to visit one another whenever we choose."

"That's how it used to be, Mother," Dawson bit back. "We could move freely between shifter realms, do as we pleased. But you seem to forget what happened. Smaller clans, like Thunder

Cove, were betrayed by that freedom. Invaded, robbed, their Alphas killed." He clenched his jaw, pausing just a moment. "There are neutral zones outside each portal, so we have no need to enter another realm without permission."

Ciara pressed her lips together and looked at Dawson, then me. "Well then..." she said, seemingly not interested in debating clan law. "I should leave you to enjoy your party."

I watched her walk toward the crowd, all eyes on her. She certainly commanded the room.

"What crawled up her ass and died?" Jasmine scrunched up her face, then shook her head and eyed the necklace. "At least she's got great taste in jewelry. I'll give her that. And *only* that."

"It suits you." Dawson leaned in, his gaze pinned to my lips. "Though its beauty pales in comparison."

I sat back under his watchful gaze, a smile plastered on my face, which matched the warmth blooming in my heart. Jasmine nudged me with her elbow.

"If that's the best pickup line he's got, you might want to tell him to work on his material."

Dawson laughed. "I better go find Richard before it gets too late," he told me, as he kissed me on the cheek. "But I won't be long."

He peered at Jasmine with a playful expression, then returned his gaze to me. "Don't let Miss Killjoy rub off on you. She loves to pretend she's all brooding and cynical, but deep down, she's a hopeless romantic."

Jasmine snorted, then shook her head.

I was still laughing when another group of women approached the table to wish me well and tell me how happy they were I was there. I was relieved Jasmine stayed by my side, helping me greet the dozens of people who welcomed me into the pack while simultaneously keeping my wine glass full.

By the end of the hour, I was on a high—my heart so full I thought it might burst.

"Hi, Ember. It's a pleasure to meet you." The voice that greeted me was as soft as honey.

When I looked up, the woman who stood before me was nothing short of stunning. She was tall and lean, with midnight-black hair that fell to her waist. She was the definition of sex on heels.

"Hi," I said with a smile. "Thank you. What's your name?"

"Isabella." Her eyes danced across my face and then swept down to my feet and back up again. For a split second, her mask slipped, her smile vanishing.

"It's nice to meet you too. I hope you're having a great time."

"I just arrived," she replied. "Where's the Alpha? I was hoping to get a moment alone with him tonight." Isabella's voice had turned sultry as though merely asking about Dawson had turned her on and she wasn't at all concerned about hiding it.

I stared at her in surprise as a surge of protectiveness washed over me, but I pushed it away.

Why did it matter to me if this striking beauty was interested in Dawson? He was the Alpha; of course, chicks would be throwing themselves at him.

"I'm not sure where he is right now," I told her, but she didn't seem to acknowledge my response. Instead, she watched me with those blazing eyes, and I returned the same intensity, a silent sparring match I wasn't so sure I could win.

When Isabella didn't say a word, or even take a step back, I finally surrendered, breaking the silence and giving her the information she seemed to know I had. "He went to speak with Richard. He should be back later."

"Thank you," Isabella responded, raking her fingers through her silky hair. "Have a good evening."

The possessive surge rattled through me again, and I bit my lip so hard I tasted blood.

Who the fuck was that girl?

"I see you've met Isabella," Jasmine told me when the conversation she'd been having with a group of girls ended and she returned her attention to me. "She's been chasing after Dawson since we were teens. Now that he's Alpha, she's trying even harder."

"She's gorgeous. I can see why he'd like her."

Jasmine snickered. "Do I sense a little jealousy?"

I opened my mouth to protest, but I knew the truth was written all over my flushed face.

Jasmine nudged me playfully. "Don't get your panties in a bunch. Isabella's not Dawson's type. Eventually, she'll give up. He's certainly made it clear he isn't interested in her."

I wanted to ask her how the hell a woman who looked like *that* could possibly not be any man's type, but I kept it to myself.

"Want to dance?" Jasmine asked me when a band appeared, playing a type of music I could only describe as Celtic meets reggae. "Or do we need to drink another glass of wine first?"

"I think I can manage it." I giggled. I was certainly not a great dancer, but before too long, I found myself surrounded by clan members and lost in the rhythm of the music. Gia, Maria, and Anita joined us, and we danced until we were out of breath.

Dawson had yet to return, but I was so caught up with enjoying myself I hadn't noticed how much time had passed. I found myself pulled in a hundred different directions, men and women wanting to welcome me and tell me everything there was to know about Silver Creek.

I learned this clan could shift whenever they wanted to, rather than just under a full moon like the members of Thunder Cove. I heard all about the many events Silver Creek celebrated throughout the year and how their winter solstice was one of the most highly anticipated of them all. But one of the things both packs had in common was there'd never been a female Alpha. The role went only to men, usually handed down to the firstborn son after the Alpha had passed on.

Finally, I plopped down into a nearby chair, out of breath

but deliriously happy. I glanced around for Dawson, but he was nowhere to be seen. I secretly hoped Isabella hadn't found him.

"No," a voice from somewhere behind me answered a question I hadn't even spoken aloud.

"Excuse me?" I asked, whirling around, but no one was there.

"No."

My breath hitched in my throat, and I could hardly move.

"No, your parents aren't here."

My eyes searched for the source, but all I found were people dancing, drinking, and celebrating. Not a single person appeared as though they'd been talking to me.

"Ember."

This time I barely heard my name over the thrum of the music, but when I turned my head, a woman stepped into view.

It was the same woman who'd visited me the night before in my room when she'd brought me clothing and the beautiful dress I'd worn to dinner.

"Who are you?" I asked, fear tightening my throat. "What do you want?"

The woman's eyes darted around as though she didn't want to be seen talking to me, but then she leaned in close and whispered into my ear, "Come with me, my child. Quickly. You're in danger here."

CHAPTER TEN

EMBER

The woman's blue eyes swirled with a sense of urgency.

"Please, come with me."

As though my body had a mind of its own, I rose to my feet as she quickly made her way through the crowded room and slipped out a side door.

My mind raced, and fear gripped my heart, but I dutifully followed. Once outside, she ushered me away from the castle.

For a moment, I wondered if I should follow her, uncertainty crawling over my skin, but the sparkle in her eyes told me she wouldn't harm me.

We headed toward an unfamiliar path, the moon above doing little to light our way. I struggled to see more than a few feet in front of my face. Unlike the night before when Dawson had taken me to see the unicorns, this area of the castle grounds was in sheer darkness.

For a split second, I nearly tripped over a root, but then the strange woman was by my side, steadying me, as we made our way through the woods. Suddenly, the rush of flowing water filled my ears. I panicked, my arms stretching out in front of me in an attempt to feel my way. The woman reached out once again, guiding me away from the shore until all I could hear was the chirp of crickets and the swish of grass under our feet.

We walked for what felt like an eternity, each step leading me farther from the castle. When we rounded another corner, dim lights glowed in the distance.

I froze, stricken with fear. If I screamed for help, no one would hear me, not this far away. Yet she was just an old woman, certainly nothing I should be afraid of. I took another step forward, deciding I'd quickly shift and race back to the castle if I sensed anything out of the ordinary.

As we came closer to the edge of the forest, a small, vine-entwined cottage finally came into view, golden light flickering behind frosted windows.

It looked like it belonged in a painting with its arched door, intricately carved woodwork, and cross-gabled, steeply pitched roof.

"Please, come inside. You'll be safe here."

I followed her into the tiny space, where a fireplace roared to life as she walked by. A table was off to the side of the room, with wooden chairs scattered around and what looked like an assortment of jars and vases strewn all over.

There was a crunch beneath my feet as I took another step, and when I glanced down, I saw I was walking over dry herbs, the sweet scent of lavender and rosemary filling my lungs.

"Take a seat, Ember. Anywhere you like."

I chose the chair closest to the door, my heart still thumping in my chest.

"Why did you bring me here?" My voice betrayed me, squeaking out the fear which rippled down my spine.

"Please, be calm. I wish you no harm."

I swallowed down my nerves, but when she stepped close to me with what appeared to be some of the same dry herbs and pressed them against my palm, my trembling fingers barely managed to hold on to them.

"You said I was in danger. What did you mean? Please, I don't understand."

"My dear girl," she said, her soothing voice easing some of the tension in the room. "You already know of the darkness which seeks you. It marked you with its wish for death. I only want to help you."

"How can you help me?"

This woman knew about my mark and that a shadow beast was after me.

How was that possible?

"To every poison, there is an anecdote, is there not? You will find yours."

I was mesmerized by the light dancing in her eyes as she spoke in riddles only she understood, yet there was wisdom in her tone.

"You can help me remove the mark? Stop the lupus interfectorem from coming for me?"

Her expression darkened, and I instantly knew I was asking for something beyond her capabilities. Whoever this woman was, she couldn't save me.

"Only *you* can do that, child," she said, taking the leaves from my palm. She set them on the table and then picked up a turquoise bottle from a shelf, dabbing a few drops of its contents onto a cloth. Then she turned her back to me, and I saw her arms moving, her hands at work pouring a drop of liquid from one vial into the next.

"But I can help you prepare for when it comes."

She instructed me to lower my head, and then I felt her rough, timeworn fingers moving my hair and exposing the back of my neck. I gasped when the cloth she was holding touched my skin. A streak of fire raced across the mark, though it quickly dulled to a mere simmer.

"Stay still. Just a few more minutes."

She held the fabric to my neck for what felt like an eternity, and then finally, she stepped back, discarding the cloth by tossing it into the fire.

I reached to the back of my neck but felt nothing.

"What was on that cloth? And why are you helping me?"

The old woman smiled as she sat in a nearby chair. She looked exhausted, as though whatever she'd done to me had zapped her of what little energy she had left. Even her skin appeared to have lost some of its color.

"You did nothing to warrant what happened to you. Please know that none of this is your fault."

I peered at her, wishing she'd tell me more. "Back at the castle, you said my parents weren't there. Do you know who they are? Where they are?"

She sighed deeply. Fatigue settled into the lines of her face, but I pressed on. If this woman had answers, I needed to hear them. The thought of possibly learning who my parents were filled me with a newfound sense of courage. There was no longer room to deny that I wanted to know them.

"Please, tell me. I need to know."

"Your parents are not here. Not at Silver Creek. I'm sorry, child, but that's all I know."

I got the sense she wasn't telling me the truth, but when I tried pushing her for more information, she seemed to grow fearful and insisted it was time for me to return to the castle, reminding me people would be looking for me.

We strolled in silence as she escorted me back through the forest, the darkness causing me to move slowly, but as the castle came into view, I reached out for her, ready to beg her to tell me more. My hands felt nothing but a gust of wind.

She was gone.

And when I slid my fingers over the mark on my neck, wondering what she'd done, I realized so was the necklace.

CHAPTER ELEVEN

EMBER

"Where did you go?" Jasmine asked me when I returned to the castle. "Dawson is looking for you. He wanted to make a speech and thank everyone for coming, but you weren't here."

"I just had to catch my breath and get some fresh air," I lied. For some reason, I didn't want to tell anyone about my run-in with the old woman. I felt guilty for leaving with her, only to discover my necklace was missing, but I also didn't want to accuse the woman just yet.

"You feeling okay? I can imagine how overwhelming this all is."

The crowd had cleared out, with only a few small groups remaining, and I was thankful for it. I felt drained. All I wanted to do was slip into bed. The thought of having lost the necklace sent a wave of anxiety through my body, and I felt myself swaying, dizzy with fear.

What would Ciara say when she discovered I no longer had her gift?

I didn't want to believe the old woman had taken it, but I also hadn't felt it slip off my neck. There had to be another explanation. As soon as the morning sun appeared, I'd retrace my steps and find it. I only hoped no one noticed it was gone before I could recover it.

"I'm fine, just tired," I answered as a yawn escaped my lips. "I'm going to find Dawson and thank him for such a wonderful night. Then I'm off to bed."

She smirked at me as though she'd uncovered a secret. "Off to bed alone? Because if Dawson has his way, he'll be joining—"

"Yes, alone," I replied. "Dawson and I are just friends." I didn't know why I was telling her this, especially when I wasn't sure it was totally true. "I'm grateful to him for bringing me here and helping me get to know my clan, but I'm not looking for a relationship. I have too many other things to deal with right now. And I just got here."

She stared at me intently and nodded slowly, but I got the sense she didn't entirely believe me. "I get that. I'm the same way. I don't want to settle down right now, and the whole barefoot-and-pregnant thing doesn't appeal to me whatsoever. In fact, the thought makes me cringe."

The flushed expression on her face told me a very different story.

"Have you ever been in love before?"

She bit her bottom lip thoughtfully, caught off guard by my question. For a moment, I didn't think she'd even answer me, but then she nodded slowly. "Once. But he's in love with someone else, and I'm fine with that. His loss."

Before I could reply, she changed the subject as if speaking about him caused her pain. "Here comes Dawson. I'm tired as well, so I'm going to head back home. I'm happy you had a great night, Ember."

"I had a wonderful night," I replied. "Thank you for helping Dawson put this together for me. You're a really good friend."

To my surprise, she leaned in and gave me a quick hug. "I wouldn't go *that* far." She giggled, her eyes sparkling. "But every so often, someone comes along who's worth the effort."

She graced me with a smile before she headed toward the door, stopping only long enough for Dawson to hug her goodbye. Then he made his way over to me.

"Well, there you are," he said. "I was looking for you everywhere. For a minute, I thought you'd ditched me." His eyes held a teasing glint.

"I'm sorry. I just needed to step out for a minute."

Part of me wished I could've evaded Dawson altogether, so he wouldn't get the chance to notice his mother's gift was no longer hanging from my neck, but I knew he'd be upset if I didn't at least say goodnight. Still, I wanted to make it as quick as possible.

"I had a great time," I told him as he nodded to a man who patted him on the shoulder before shuffling out the door. "Thank you for everything."

"It was my pleasure, though I was hoping the night wouldn't end so soon. I haven't gotten nearly enough of you." His lips curved into something halfway between a smile and a smirk that made a blush creep up my cheeks.

"Ember, welcome home," a woman told me as she walked by.

"I told you, you had nothing to worry about," Dawson said as another stopped to greet me.

"Alpha, I hate to interrupt, but can I speak to you?"

I turned to find Craig standing in the doorway. He grinned at me, then nodded to Dawson. "We've received news about our upcoming meeting."

Dawson's expression gave nothing away. Whether it was good or bad news, I couldn't know, but when his gaze returned to me, I thought I caught a glimpse of disappointment. Then he blinked, and his sexy smirk was back.

"Head over to the tavern. I'll meet you and the others for a drink when I'm finished here. I've got a matter that needs tending to first."

"Yes, Alpha," Craig said, a knowing look on his face that I

wasn't following. "See you soon." He tipped his head to me and bid me goodnight before he disappeared from the room, leaving only Dawson and me plus a few members of the band who were packing their instruments away.

"A matter that needs tending to? Is everything okay?"

"Everything is perfect," Dawson told me. "Just give me one second. I'll be right back."

He strode over to a stout man who stood at least six feet tall and whispered something in his ear. As the man pulled his guitar from its case, I recognized him as being an extraordinarily gifted musician from earlier in the night.

As if by magic, the lights dimmed so we were illuminated only by candlelight. Then Dawson was standing before me, his hand outstretched and a sly grin on his face.

"I never got the chance to dance with you," he murmured, his raspy voice a seductive kiss as his eyes locked on mine and the music began to play. "Will you do me the honor?"

"I don't know how to do this," I squeaked when his hand captured mine, and he pulled me against him.

I felt like I had two left feet, worried I'd step on his toes, but he guided me gracefully, his hands never leaving mine.

"When I left the human realm," he whispered against my cheek, referencing the day we'd met. "I couldn't get you off my mind." His voice was dangerously low. "I came home to a great loss. I said goodbye to my father, and I thought my world would fall apart…but then I thought about you. And somehow, I knew we'd meet again."

I closed my eyes as his voice purred against my skin. A wave of heat slid over my chest, tightening my nipples into hard buds. There was so much emotion in his tone, so much depth to what he told me that it made my pulse race and my knees weak.

For a moment, as he held me in his arms, I forgot about having lost the necklace and the strange things the old woman had told me.

It was just him and me, lost in the song and the growing bond between us.

"I'm glad we did," I told him. "I'm so happy to be here with you."

He leaned down, nuzzling my ear and breathing deeply before letting a hot whisper caress my neck. "This is the song I heard every time I thought of you. It played in my head—this sweet melody which reminded me there was someone out there who made me feel things I'd never felt before."

I didn't know what to say. Since my wolf had surfaced, I'd begun to understand how much emotion our kind could feel. The walls which had guarded my heart for so many years had no chance against the primal connection between a she-wolf and someone as captivating as Dawson.

But I refused to forget the men who'd saved my life, who'd brought me into this world, and who'd shown me kindness. I wasn't here in Silver Creek to fall in love with someone else. I was here to fall in love with *myself*, to discover who I was meant to be, to let my wolf thrive amongst her own.

"Ember, I'd never let you want for anything—no pleasure, no small desire...nothing your heart or body wanted would go unfulfilled. I'd give anything—"

His voice broke, and a small sob had me wiping my tears.

"Dawson... I'm grateful to you for everything you've done. For bringing me home, for being so kind to me. But—"

"I know, and I'm sorry. I don't want to pressure you. It isn't fair." His breath tickled the hair along my hairline, and his lips brushed my ear. "But I have this now."

I hazarded a glance at his face. His eyes darkened into pools of silvery hunger.

"I have you here for this moment." His breathless words were laced with need. "And right now, that's enough for me."

The song ended, but the flutter of my heart continued well into the night.

He pressed a lingering kiss to my lips. "Want me to walk you to your room before I go find Craig?"

"I think I can find my way. I've held you up long enough."

"I love every moment I get to spend with you." He squeezed my hand. "Get some rest and I'll see you in the morning."

"Thanks for tonight," I called over my shoulder as I headed off in the direction of my room.

Even when I finally laid my head on my pillow and closed my eyes, the voice in my head refused to be silent.

I thought about Grayson...and Alex...and Cody. And Dawson.

When I left Thunder Cove, I knew I couldn't look back—at least not until I'd figured out a way to defeat the shadow realm —but my heart didn't beat the same without them.

And now I was here with Dawson, a man who wasn't afraid to tell me how he felt. He didn't care if it was too soon or that we barely knew each other. And he was the Alpha of Silver Creek, my family.

Then my thoughts drifted into darker waters.

A mark on the back of my neck tied me to the shadow realm. The old woman had told me there was an anecdote for every poison and I'd find mine. But I didn't know where to begin looking or how I'd ever save myself.

I had to tell him. I had to tell Dawson the truth.

I blinked back tears at how hopeless things seemed. One day, another creature would come calling for me, to claim my soul and reap its reward.

The only question was, how much time did I have left?

CHAPTER TWELVE

ALEX

"I need to talk to Ember," Selena told me, her eyes wild and her arms heavy with books. "I went by Cody's house, but he wasn't home. Is she here?"

It looked as though she hadn't slept, and I was instantly on edge, having never seen her like that before.

"It's important. Please, Alex! Where is she?"

"What is it, Selena? What's going on?"

I stepped to the side, ushering her in. I needed her to relax and tell me what was going on, but she remained rooted in place, her body quivering.

"No, I don't have time to come in. I need to talk to Ember right now!"

"Selena, please, calm down." I pulled her arm, nearly knocking the books out of her hands as I practically dragged her inside with me. "Ember is gone, and I don't think she's coming back."

Saying those words out loud made it all too real, and my heart grew heavy.

"I've been researching ever since I took Ember to meet Elgin.

And I discovered something," she continued, her voice cracking. "Something about the lupus interfectorem."

I glanced up sharply. "You brought Ember to meet Elgin and no one told me?"

"That's my fault. Ember wanted to tell you. I told her not to," Selena said. "Anyway, he told us that as long as she's marked, the shadow realm will keep sending beasts after her. But I found something that might help."

"What did you find?" I asked, my pulse quickening.

Before she could tell me, Rylen entered the room and took a seat next to me.

"Is everything okay?" he asked.

I shook my head, my gaze locked on Selena's frantic face. "Selena, please sit. Tell me what you've learned."

She sank down across from us, her books still clutched in her arms. Leaning over, she set all but one on the floor.

"I've been researching everything I could find about the shadow realm," she told us, her fingers flipping through the thin pages of an ancient tome so quickly I was sure the fragile paper would crumble under her touch. "At first, I couldn't find anything useful. Just a bit about the history of the shadow realm, but nothing stood out."

"Why are you researching the shadow realm?" Rylen asked her.

My body grew tense when he looked at me, his eyes filled with accusation.

We hadn't shared that Ember had been attacked by a lupus interfectorem with Rylen, nor had we told him everything we'd discovered since. We'd kept the information close to our chests so as to not cause chaos within the clan, but as Rylen's posture stiffened, it was clear he was piecing it together.

"Ember…is she marked?" Rylen clenched his jaw and waited for me to respond.

I stared him dead in the eye, making it clear he needed to

keep his temper in check when I finally told him all that we knew. I wouldn't tolerate an outburst from our beta. But before I could say a word, Selena found whatever she was looking for and jumped up.

"This," she exclaimed, her pitch rising. "Look at this."

She held out the open book, pointing to a page of text. I reached out and pulled the tome into my hands, my gaze zeroing in on what she was trying to show me.

It was in another language. "What does it say?"

I studied the foreign words, trying to make sense of the faded text. When I peered up at Selena, who was back on her feet, pacing the room, it was clear she'd somehow translated whatever it was.

"Eye of the moon," she replied excitedly. "The words are Latin. I had to find someone who could read the old language."

She knelt on the floor next to my feet and peeked down at the pages, pointing a finger at the passage. "It's a relic of some kind which was broken into two pieces a long time ago. Centuries."

"What else does the script say?"

"He couldn't make out most of it," she told us. "But he said whoever holds the eye of the moon controls its power."

It was no surprise that even someone fluent in Latin would struggle to translate the text. The ink was so distressed and worn in some places it was barely noticeable.

"But what does this have to do with the lupus interfectorem?" I asked her.

Selena's eyes lit up, the expression on her face sparking hope. "When the two pieces are placed together, it gives the holder power over the shadow realm."

A tingle licked up my spine, and I shivered. "What kind of power?"

Selena's shoulders sank. "That I don't know. He couldn't make out the rest, and I can't find any other reference to it." She gazed up at me, tears glistening in her eyes. "But it's something. It could help Ember. We need to tell her."

"We can't." I paused, watching the confusion cross her face. "We don't know where she is. Cody tried to find her, but her scent disappears just outside our territory."

"The fucking halfling is marked," Rylen muttered to himself, his expression even grimmer than before.

"Yes, Rylen, she is," Selena replied candidly. "And she needs our help."

Rylen's features tugged into a scowl, and the glimmer of annoyance in his eyes was replaced with searing-hot anger. "What are you fucking talking about? Help her? The shadow realm could've wiped us out! We would've never survived a full-on attack."

"You're an asshole," Selena said, her expression instantly hardening. "Ember is innocent in all this. We *need* to help her. If we don't, she'll never survive."

"Ember isn't part of our clan," Rylen hissed between clenched teeth. "What part of that aren't you understanding? We *aren't* responsible for her. You can't expect our Alphas to leave their realm and go searching for her. They have hundreds of people here to care for, to protect."

"How can you be so heartless?" Selena lashed out. "She's a shifter who was marked by a fucking wolf slayer. If we don't help her, who will?"

Rylen took a deep breath, clearly wrestling with his desire to roar at the top of his lungs. "That's not our problem. It's a good thing she's no longer here."

I looked at Rylen sharply, my body stiffening, his words like needles under my skin. "*We* brought her into this world," I told him as Selena got to her feet, her eyes burning with determination now that she knew I was in agreement. "Ember may not be part of our clan, but she *is* our responsibility. And we need to find her."

Grayson was right. And so was Cody. Ember needed our help, whether she belonged to our pack or not. As dangerous as it might be, and as risky, the truth was our hearts were at the mercy of the blue-eyed girl who'd taught us so much more about ourselves than she'd ever know.

And as I instructed Rylen to watch over the clan while we were away, I knew I'd do anything I could to help free Ember from the control the shadow realm held over her.

Even if it meant waging war on Silver Creek.

CHAPTER THIRTEEN

EMBER

I woke as a brilliant streak of sunshine poured through my bedroom window. A few minutes later, I was outside, headed in the same direction as the night before, trying to retrace my steps.

As promised, I gave my wolf free rein to roam, setting my clothes aside, then quickly looking around so I could find a marker for when I needed to return to them.

I lowered to the soft ground, my knees planted firmly in the grass as I began to shift. As always, the sensation of the transformation was all-consuming, every muscle stretching to impossible lengths before forming into the powerful body of a wolf.

She yelped in appreciation as I took off running, my paws barely touching the ground as I headed toward the fields.

But the farther I got from the castle, the more confused I became when there was no cottage in sight, nor was there even a beaten path. The grounds ahead looked like nothing more than miles of vibrant green grass with shades of gold, some patches almost five feet tall.

I spun around, trying to figure out which way to go, but when nothing looked familiar, I randomly chose a direction, then another, as I ran through miles of field, only to come up short.

The cottage was nowhere to be found.

Exhausted and overheated, I nearly howled in frustration, plopping myself on the ground to take a much-needed break.

Think, Ember.

I closed my eyes and thought about the route the old woman had taken. It was pitch dark when she'd guided me along the path through the dense forest. I'd nearly tripped over a root, and then I'd heard the sound of rushing water.

I couldn't see above the tall grass when in my true form, so to my wolf's dismay, I shifted back. The process was faster than before, and I realized the more often I transformed, the more control I had over it.

Once complete, I stood naked, surveying the landscape, searching for a river, brook, creek, anything that would help give me some sense of direction. I pushed through the tall grass as I made my way, headed toward an area I hadn't yet covered. And then another. Finding nothing but miles of open space, tall grass, and orchards, heavy with fruit.

Hours later, as the sun began to dip below the horizon, I stopped in my tracks. Off in the distance came the wail of a loon, its haunting call guiding me along. As I crested a hill, I saw it.

The cottage didn't look the same in the dwindling light of the sun. The roof was sagging as though it might tumble down at the slightest gust of wind, and the windows were cracked and yellowed.

I stepped closer, noticing how the path beneath my feet was untouched, without even the faintest sign of our footsteps from the night before. And when I finally made my way to the front door, I found it stuck, its hinges so rusty I could barely crack it open.

Once inside, I stayed close to the entryway, my eyes taking

in the sight of the ransacked room, my mind unable to believe what was before me.

It looked nothing like the night before. No dried herbs littered the floor. No colorful bottles filled with liquids lined the shelves. There wasn't even a single chair to be found, nor was there a fireplace against the far wall. The room was completely bare, its floorboards rotted and gray. When I dared to take a step forward, I squealed as a rat scurried from a hole in the wall.

None of it made sense. I'd just been to this place hours ago. Despite how impossibly different the cottage appeared, I was sure this was where the woman had taken me.

I glanced around the tiny room one last time, not daring to venture beyond the entrance, and when I was satisfied that the necklace wasn't there, I headed back outside, my lungs relishing in the fresh air.

When I looked up, dark clouds had turned the sky a murky gray, and a crescent moon took shape above me. Off in the distance, thunder rumbled. I shifted and then took off, running in the direction where I'd stashed my clothing.

Life had become one giant obstacle, with one step forward, then two steps back. Nothing made sense anymore.

Back in human form, I returned to the castle in search of Dawson. It was time to tell him everything and ask the clan for help in finding a way to defeat the shadow realm. I refused to live life constantly looking over my shoulder, always wondering when the next creature would come for me.

I headed for the Great Hall, hoping Dawson would be there, perhaps in a meeting. But when I entered the massive room, it was empty. Even the decorations and tables had been put away.

I rested my back against the wall, taking a deep breath and thinking about exactly what I was going to say when I found him.

I pushed away from the wall, determined to get this over

with. But as I headed for the door, I saw the old woman walk by. My heart jumped into my throat.

"Hey!" I shouted, rushing after her as she disappeared through a door a short distance from the Great Hall. I followed, determined to confront her, to demand that she tell me everything she knew.

"Who are you?" I asked her when I cornered her in a room.

"I'm just a servant," she replied. "I've worked in this castle for many years. I serve my Alpha and the Alphas before."

I shook my head, refusing to accept her answer. "You're *more* than that. That stuff you put on my neck. What was it?"

Her eyes flickered to the door behind me. It was clear she didn't want anyone to hear our conversation.

I lowered my voice, "Tell me everything you know. I went to your cottage…"

This time her gaze found mine, and I saw fear burning in their depths.

"It was as though no one had lived there for many years. But last night, when you brought me there—"

"Please," she begged me. "Don't speak of this here. I only tried to help you. But if anyone finds out I used magic—"

"Magic?" My eyes widened as realization set in. I thought about the dried herbs on the cottage floor and the assortment of colorful bottles on the shelves. "You're a witch. And you used a potion on me."

She nodded slowly. "This realm doesn't allow the use of magic, but I did what I could to help you. The potion will weaken the shadow realm's hold on you. But that was all I could do. One witch cannot undo what another has done."

"What's your name?" For some reason, it seemed important that I know. "Please, tell me."

"Ravena," she whispered, her eyes darting up to the ceiling as though she heard something.

"Ravena," I echoed, my gaze transfixed on her face. "Did you take the necklace Ciara gave me?"

She gave a slight bob of her head, and I could see the fear in her eyes.

"I won't tell anyone. I promise." The words slipped out of my mouth without thought, but they were true. Something about this woman made me want to keep her secrets. "You can trust me."

Ravena nodded slowly as she pondered what I'd said.

"I need to know why you took it. If you need money, I'm sure Dawson would help you."

She regarded me for a moment; her gaze tinged with sadness as she studied me in silence. Then her expression changed. Fear still traced the curve of her face, but there was something else— a softness, and I hoped for a crack in her resistance to tell me all she knew.

"I don't need money," Ravena replied, her voice clear and firm. "I was only trying to help you. I—"

Her eyes grew distant as she stared right through me, and I cleared my throat.

"Ravena, what is it?"

She sniffed, the rhythm of our conversation broken when she turned away.

"It's coming."

My brows furrowed. "What's coming?"

But as soon as the words escaped my lips, I knew the answer to my question. The reason all the color had drained from her face, turning it a ghostly white.

She headed for the door, and I followed close behind as we made our way out into the courtyard.

Once outside, Ravena pointed off in the distance, her eyes growing impossibly wide. "It's coming."

"What do I do?" I peered around in confusion as fear rattled through my body. I didn't know if I should run, and if so, in what direction.

"Don't give in to its call," Ravena told me, repeating herself when I failed to answer. "You can fight it. You're strong enough."

Screams tore through the air as a handful of pack members ran from an enemy they sensed but couldn't see. Above all that, I heard the distinctive screech I knew all too well.

A sound I'd only heard once before but hadn't forgotten.

Wolf slayer.

CHAPTER FOURTEEN

EMBER

My pulse spiked, and I felt lightheaded as the realization set in that my greatest fear was happening. My nightmare was coming back to life.

But I didn't scream for help, nor did I call out for Dawson. The darkness had followed me here, as I knew it would. Now I had to face it, no matter what happened.

"Ember!" Dawson's voice was filled with panic as he made his way toward me.

I wanted to tell him to stay away from me, to protect his clan and not risk his life against the evil lurking in the shadows. But when he appeared just a few feet away, whatever bravery I thought I had shattered into a million pieces. I nearly sobbed when he stood in front of me protectively.

"What is that?" His eyes darted around, searching for the source of what was now a low, endless growl. His expression changed to one of knowing, and he stared back at me, a shadow crossing his face. "Dark magic. My mother—"

Whatever he was going to say died on his lips when the beast emerged, its crimson eyes sending a chill down my spine and made the hairs on my arms stand up.

"Dawson, I'm sorry. I wanted to tell you. I thought I'd have more time."

He didn't look back at me, nor did he question what I was trying to say. Instead, he stood firm, steadfast in the face of danger as though he hadn't heard me at all.

The creature sniffed the air, searching for me, and then its vicious gaze locked on to my face like a sniper who'd found its mark.

"Alpha, move back!"

I recognized the voice as belonging to Craig. As a sea of men appeared behind him, their weapons ready, I prayed we'd survive the fight.

The beast stared at me as though I was the only person standing in the courtyard. As it snaked closer, the thrum of its power invaded my senses. My wolf howled at me to back off, to shift and run as fast as I could, but when I tried to tap into that primal energy, I couldn't.

Then I heard it. For the first time, the beast spoke to me. *"You belong to me,"* it growled as it breathed in my scent.

It lifted its inky arms. Shadows swirled as though parts of its very body had detached itself and transformed into a heavy cloud of darkness which filled the air with a putrid stench.

"Ember, you bear our mark," the beast bellowed. *"And I've come to claim what is ours."*

My lungs burned as I choked on the thick smoke cloaking me in its suffocating embrace. When I dared to look back, I saw that Dawson and his men were oddly rooted in place. He appeared to be struggling to step forward and reach out to me, but something prevented him from doing so. The dark magic had created a barricade between us.

"Ember!" Dawson called out to me, his voice edged in powerless desperation, but I was helpless to resist the call from the monster.

Don't give in to its call.

Ravena's words suddenly surfaced in my mind as though she was standing next to me, but when my gaze darted around frantically in search of her, she was nowhere to be found.

Don't give in to its call.

The mark on the back of my neck suddenly grew hot the closer I got to the beast, the connection tugging me along as though I was nothing more than a marionette and the darkness my puppet master.

Suddenly, a wicked vein of lightning struck the cast iron rooster on the east tower, sending sparks showering down like a firework display which highlighted the dark figure perched in stone below.

When I'd first seen it upon entering this realm, I'd looked at it as nothing more than a creepy ornament attached to the castle, but now I wished with all my heart the gargoyle would come to life and save us all.

Dawson's voice called again, fainter than before, as though it took every bit of strength for him to get his words to reach me beyond the shadowy barricade. He was begging for me to turn back, but I was crippled against the beast's pull. It was as though my body now belonged to it.

A deep rumble came from the creature again, and its mouth curved into a satisfied grin. I was almost within its reach. The trancelike sensation of being powerless crawled over my skin. While terror bloomed in my chest when it lifted a razor-sharp claw and beckoned me closer, I couldn't stop my feet from betraying me as I took another step forward.

"What do you want from me? Please, let me go."

It didn't answer, but it kept its hateful gaze trained on my face as it drew me even closer. The heat of its rancid breath washed over my face, but all I could do was close my eyes and accept my fate.

Then it happened—the beating sound of wings reached my ears. My eyes flew open as I tried to understand what was happening. The monster was too caught up with me to notice when a streak of movement appeared high up in the night sky. Within seconds the streak came closer, suddenly fluttering its mighty wings just a few feet above.

"Don't give in to its call."

Off in the distance, I saw the silhouette of a woman standing by the path which led to the portal. She lifted her arms, and the gargoyle flew higher, then as her arms dropped, so did the stone body, its giant wings thrashing against the dark creature.

The beast stumbled back in confusion. In those few seconds, I tapped into a power I didn't know I had, and the connection was lost—whatever hold it had over me temporarily fading.

"A witch," Dawson growled from behind me; the barricade finally weakened, allowing him to move forward. "A witch brought this creature into our realm."

"No," I replied, my gaze locked on the woman's form.

While her profile was barely visible in the shadows, I knew it had to be Ravena. I watched, in awe, as she commanded the gargoyle to attack the creature again.

"She's helping us, Dawson. She's on our side."

I dropped to my knees and let my wolf take over, knowing I'd be stronger in my true form. She howled with delight as she surfaced, and when I glanced back, I saw that Dawson and his men had also transformed.

"Ember, no. You need to get into the castle and barricade the entrance."

"I have to fight this," I replied. *"It won't stop coming for me."*

Dawson's eyes widened in confusion. He didn't know I'd been marked. But as my words reached him, it was clear he finally understood. I'd put him and his clan in grave danger, and now there was nothing I could do about it now but take a stand and fight.

I stared off in the distance, searching for Ravena, but she was nowhere to be seen. The gargoyle was still attacking the creature, but it was apparent it wouldn't be able to hold it off for long.

"Move forward!" Dawson's voice was firm, not so much as a quiver in his tone, as he commanded his men to attack. He may not have wanted the role, but at that moment, there was no denying he was a born leader.

Craig lunged forward, his legs kicking up dirt as he and his men raced toward the monster.

"Please, Ember. Let us handle this."

"No," I replied. *"I need to be here."*

"Then we'll destroy it together."

I felt a surge of strength and determination greater than I'd ever felt before as I ran toward the beast. Craig and his men were already on it, their teeth ripping at the beast's flesh.

It shrieked, the piercing sound rising above the howls, as it scrambled to locate me in the horde. It didn't seem to care it was being attacked by a pack of fierce wolves and a gargoyle who continued to assault it from above. Its only desire was to claim the soul of the one who bore its mark.

I sank my fangs into its leg, growling as the taste of death coated my tongue. My bite seemed to make no difference in taking down the creature, though my touch seemed to be all it needed to locate me.

It rose to what seemed like an impossible height. I howled in horror as wolves lost their grip and spiraled to the ground below, Dawson amongst them.

"Ember, be careful!"

I clung to my monster, refusing to let go, even when it flung its ghostly arms into the air and knocked the gargoyle to the ground, smashing its stone body into a hundred pieces.

Then I took a breath for bravery and attacked again, this time sinking my fangs into its arm and ripping away at anything I came in contact with. The beast refused to give up, lurching forward as it tried to free my jaws from its flesh. For a second, it felt hopeless.

Then, as I dodged the beast's deadly talons, the memory of that night in the forest surfaced, and I thought about how Grayson, Alex, and Cody had fought a creature just like this and saved my life.

I blinked back tears as their handsome, smiling faces took shape as though they were standing right in front of me. I latched on to the memory like a cherished photograph, keeping it in the center of my mind and drawing strength from it.

"I had to live to see them again."

Moving higher, I dug my claws into the beast's form and positioned myself so I was mere inches from its throat, waiting for the opportunity to attack.

I heard Dawson's howl before I realized he'd charged the beast, tackling it to the ground. When it temporarily lost its footing, I saw my moment.

I lunged at the beast's throat, my jaws widening as my fangs sank into it, refusing to let go. It shrieked and tried to shake me off, but Dawson and his men attacked it from the ground, causing it to lose its balance once again while I kept my hold on it, adrenaline streaking through my veins. I shook my head, my teeth gouging deeper until the life left its body. Only then did I let go.

It tumbled to the earth, taking me with it. I quickly rolled out of the way as its body collapsed and finally went limp.

Dawson scrambled over to me and buried his muzzle into my neck.

"You did it. You destroyed the beast."

"We did it," I corrected him as we stood side by side, his paw on my back.

His men moved closer, surrounding the corpse, watching it turn to smoke until all that was left was a pile of ash.

"You're one of the strongest she-wolves I've ever seen," Craig told

me, his gaze locked on the remnants of the creature. Then his hazel eyes anchored on to Dawson as he moved to his side. *"A mate fit for an Alpha."*

With that, he and his men left us alone, the heavy pads of their paws kicking up dirt as they dashed back to the castle, but then veered left and headed for the surrounding forest.

"I won't see him until morning." Dawson chuckled as he nuzzled against me once again. *"His wolf always needs to run after a battle."*

"I feel like I'm at my strongest," I replied, fully understanding Craig's need to race through the wilderness. *"Even more so than the night of the Fallen Moon."*

And I did. Power and adrenaline raged through my body. At that moment, I felt like I could defeat anything that came my way.

I'd stared death in the face and somehow came out a victor.

My wolf was bursting with pride. When I looked up at the moon, she let out a howl so loud it echoed through the trees, upsetting a flock of broad-winged hawks who returned my cry with a high-pitched whistle of their own.

"I'll need to call a meeting with the clan. Not many witnessed this, but word will spread quickly. I'll need to address it, to prepare everyone. But not now. It can wait until morning."

Dawson nudged me lovingly before he began the transformation back to his human form, and I followed suit, though my wolf practically begged to stay in her form for just a while longer.

"Tomorrow," I promised her. *"We'll run as far as you wish tomorrow."*

But tonight, we needed to rejoice in our victory and to quench my overwhelming need for the man who'd helped me slay my demon.

I ran hand in hand with Dawson, our naked bodies glistening with sweat by the time we'd made our way through the long halls of the castle and into the privacy of his bedroom.

There was no desire to talk things out right then and no promises to be made. I knew he had questions, so many questions, but they could wait until morning. Tonight, we just needed each other, to rejoice in our victory and to celebrate being alive.

At least for one more night.

CHAPTER FIFTEEN

EMBER

"I need to feel your body," Dawson whispered against my skin as he ran his fingers over my collarbone, then across my neck, to the curve of my breasts. His gaze lit me on fire as he swept it over my face, then lower to my breasts. "This is *exactly* what I need."

I moaned at the raw edge in his voice as he pulled me closer. His lips were soft, his tongue sliding against mine as his arms banded tightly around my waist. I wanted to tell him I was in love with three other men and I wasn't free to be his. But as his fingers weaved into my hair, primal desire overtook me, and I pressed against him, my words caught in my throat.

"*You*," he murmured when he briefly let me go before scooping me into his arms and lifting me from the floor, "are exactly what I need."

I nuzzled against him, my lips finding his again, which incited a growl. I peppered soft kisses across his jaw, his scruff harsh against my mouth, but I didn't care. I wanted to taste every bit of him. I was on a high after slaying the beast. I felt as though I'd finally taken control of my life.

But despite how handsome Dawson was and how my body

hummed under his expert touch, he wasn't the only one who'd stolen my heart.

"Dawson," I whispered as guilt overtook me. "I'm in love with Grayson...and with Alex. And Cody."

I let out a gasp when he roughly set me on the bed and climbed on top of me. He reached down and gently touched my cheek, then ran his fingers across my lips. A streak of fire ran down my spine at the softness of his caress and from the way he looked at me, ever so intently.

"Is that so?" he asked, but it was clear from the look on his face he somehow already knew. "In love with the wolves of Thunder Cove, huh?"

His sexy grin did something funny to my insides. I tried to fight against my desire, to tell him that, yes, I loved them all.

"You know, even before we ever touched, I felt a connection to you." His eyes burned with barely restrained passion, but he didn't kiss me, didn't touch me this time. "It was as though you'd called me over to your stand that day at the carnival."

I smirked and raised my head from his bed, wanting to make contact, to feel the heat of his body, and to hush him. But he pulled away. He wasn't done talking.

"You have a terrible memory," I huffed, flopping back onto the pillow, though there was little power behind my words, only deep longing. "I was appalled by you and your—"

"My what?" he asked me, his voice carrying an undertone of a growl which fluttered up my thighs. "I was honest with you then, and I always will be, whether you like it or not. Besides, I was right. You are destined for greater things than anything the human realm could've offered."

"Is that so?" I licked my parched lips, wishing he'd wet them with his instead, but he seemed to be enjoying tormenting me. "Destined for greater things...sounds like you've read one too many fantasy novels."

He shot me a disarming grin that tightened my core. "I knew

you were in love with them," he told me, returning his attention to my confession. "When you first mentioned their names, it was painted all over your face." He lowered his mouth just long enough to slide his lips across my neck. Then he moved away again. "And such a beautiful face it is."

I squirmed on the bed, lifting my hips in an attempt to meet his, but he shifted ever so slightly, just out of my reach.

"And what exactly am I destined for, Dawson?" I pressed my palm against his abdomen, feeling his hard abs. I needed to find comfort in his embrace, to release this overflowing energy which burned through my body. Just for this one night. "What is my calling in life?"

"You may have feelings for those men," he replied, and when I opened my mouth to protest, to tell him that it was more than just feelings, he placed his fingers over my lips to silence me. "I believe you, and that's okay with me. But, Ember, you asked me what you're destined to be, and I'm trying to answer your question."

"I did ask," I whispered when he moved his hand away, though one finger ghosted my bottom lip. "But you seem to love talking in circles."

He smirked, then lifted my arms above my head and pinned them against the bed with one hand while his free hand played along the insides of my thighs.

"You're destined to be *mine*."

Desire curled me in hot tendrils, and I cried out, begging to feel the weight of him on me, to grind against him, to feel his cock claim my pussy.

"I'm yours for just tonight; then I'm leaving." It was the truth, and there'd be no changing my mind. "So, fuck me, Dawson. I need you."

He shook his head slowly, his gaze growing in intensity. His hard cock pressed against my thigh. It was clear he wanted it as much as I did, so why was he torturing me so?

"Not interested in just fucking you," he growled, deep and slow. "Say it. Say it for me, Ember."

I closed my eyes, trying to snuff out the scorching heat burning between my legs, begging for release. I didn't understand what Dawson wanted from me, what he wanted me to say, but now wasn't the time for guessing games. Adrenaline still raced through my veins from defeating the wolf slayer. I needed Dawson inside of me. *Now.*

"I don't know what you mean," I whispered frantically, arching my back, trying to seduce him into just bearing down on me. Maybe if my breasts were in his face, he'd stop talking.

"Tell me what you really want. I need to hear it." He gazed down at me, fire dancing in his eyes and hunger on his breath, then lowered his body to mine.

I nearly howled with relief that I'd finally be able to quench the insatiable thirst I had for this man, but rather than bury his cock inside of me, he dragged his mouth across my cheek, then down to my ear.

"Tell me." His voice was a growl against my skin. "I don't want to fuck you. Not this first time. You know what I want to do. So, tell me to do it."

I cried out when his teeth grazed my neck before his mouth claimed mine again. This time he kissed the breath out of me, refusing to stop until I was moaning into his mouth, begging for his cock—for his fingers—for *anything* that would ease the pressure.

"Dawson," I whimpered when he finally released me from the kiss. "Yes…please."

"Please…what?"

His lips curved into a wicked grin, and a streak of lightning tore up my spine and crawled its way across my chest. My nipples ached to be sucked, my clit humming with the need to be touched.

I closed my eyes once again, lost in the heat between us, the current so intense it nearly took my breath away. When I opened my eyes again, I finally understood what he was asking for.

There was sex. Hard, primal sex which reduced us to nothing but animals. That was what I'd always had. It was easier for me to fuck than to allow a man to...

"Make love to me." Tears sprang to my eyes as I heard myself whisper the words I'd only said once before. Words I knew he wanted to hear, but until I'd said them, I hadn't realized it was what I also wanted.

Alex's face suddenly took shape in my mind, and I nearly wept at the memory of his gentle caress while Cody had kissed me. Grayson, oh my gorgeous Grayson, the taste of danger every girl longed for.

And now there was Dawson, a man I craved just as much as the others.

How could I claim to have feelings for so many men? How was this possible for me?

Dawson's hands on my curves brought me back to the present. As he reached under me and squeezed my ass, I gave in to the tides of desperate need that swept me away.

"Just for tonight," I murmured.

I wasn't sure why I wanted Dawson so much. Perhaps the need to taste him, and to feel him, came from the connection I'd felt when he'd joined me in fighting the beast. He'd been unwavering in his determination, fearless in the face of danger, and it had more than turned me on.

I spread my legs for him. He shifted just enough so his cock slid over my thigh, the heat and weight of it causing me to moan against his chest in anticipation.

"You're so fucking beautiful. Just perfect."

"Oh my God," I breathed out as he kissed me softly, gently, and slowly slid his cock inside of me.

My pussy was so hot, so wet, and the sensation of being filled so completely made me cry out again.

He whimpered against my lips as he thrust against me, and it was the sexiest sound a man could make—the deliciously satisfying sound of being pleasured, of being deep inside a woman.

I wanted to make him moan like that again. And again.

He thrust his hips forward in an easy motion, his cock sliding in and out of me as his hands and mouth explored my body—his caresses gentle but firm. His hands filled with my curves as though he couldn't get enough.

"You feel amazing. So tight…so warm." His lips were nearly on mine.

I could feel their soft flutter as he spoke, barely brushing against me.

I admired the way his muscles flexed and rippled beneath my touch. His body was lean and muscular, like a runner who spent hours a day training for a marathon. When he stroked his cock inside of me again, even deeper this time, I prayed he had the stamina of a runner too.

Because I never wanted this to end.

"Oh, Dawson. Oh my God."

I wasn't much of a talker during sex, but this man made me want to scream his name until my throat was raw, made me want to beg him never to stop.

His mouth found mine once again, and this time when he kissed me, with the smooth stroke of his cock claiming my pussy, somehow it felt different. It wasn't a kiss of urgency, though it held just as much passion as before. But as he pressed his lips against mine and I opened my mouth to him, it was somehow softer, as though every brush of his lips and his tongue meant something…meant something more than flowery words or the sweet whispers of a lover ever could. It was sensual, searching, like we were both discovering something new.

I closed my eyes and let him take me where he wanted to—a place of complete surrender, and at that moment, it was just the two of us.

"Baby," he whispered against my breast before his mouth claimed it. "I want you on top of me."

He rolled us over, so I was sitting on his lap, his cock still buried deep inside me. I loved the power I felt with every swerve of my hips. He was at my mercy, but I had no desire to tease him. I only wanted to take all he had to offer and give just as much of myself in return.

I shifted forward, my body sliding over his, my hips grinding down, as my hands tangled in his hair, pulling his face toward mine and kissing him with reckless abandon.

"Dawson…"

I loved the way his name tasted on my lips as I slid against him, his cock fueling me on with every hard, full stroke as the ache inside me deepened. I hardly dared to take a breath. I was so close to the edge, and when he pulled my chest against his so he could kiss me once again, I went to the place of no return.

I cried out as an orgasm ripped through me, and my pussy tightened around his cock. He muffled my moans with his mouth. His arms were banded tightly around me.

Then I felt it, the final strokes of his cock as he too let himself go, and I squeezed out of his arms before it was too late, tumbling alongside him. He closed his eyes, his jaw clenched tight and his face flush with color as I stroked him to climax, forcing him to come for me.

He growled my name as his cock pulsated in my hand, and then he was lost in his own pleasure, his head falling back against the pillow, his perfectly muscled body sated. For now.

I snuggled against him as his fingers tangled in my hair, and he kissed my forehead.

"That was everything," he murmured, his eyes still shut as he tried to catch his breath. "You make me feel so alive."

I had no words for him as I traced lazy circles over his chest and thought about my time in Thunder Cove and then my time at Silver Creek. But as my fingertips swept over his skin, I suddenly noticed several sets of faint, jagged lines mottled across his chest.

I knew what those lines meant, I'd seen them dotted across the arm of a foster kid who'd been punished with scalding water.

"What happened?" I whispered.

Dawson brushed my hand away, then turned on his side so my back was snuggled against him, one arm draped across my hip.

"The other night, when we kissed, is this what you were trying to tell me about? About the shadow realm?" he asked, confirming the fact he wasn't interested in talking about his past. He only wanted to talk about mine. "When did it happen? And how?"

I took a deep breath and explained to him all that had happened. How a creature in the human realm had attacked me. How Cody, Grayson, and Alex had saved me. How I'd discovered I'd been marked. Dawson stayed silent, allowing me to get everything out, and only when I was finished did he speak.

"You should've told me right away," he told me, though his tone carried no anger. "Our clan will always protect one another. You'll never have to face one of those creatures alone."

I hadn't realized I was crying until I felt my cheeks grow wet, but Dawson reached out and wiped the moisture away. "Is there anything else you need to tell me?"

I thought about Ravena and how she'd helped me. The potion she'd placed on my mark had given me the strength to fight the beast's call, to fight against the pull. Had it not been for her, I wouldn't have stood a chance against such a monster.

But then I thought about the fear in her eyes when she'd confessed to using magic, and I wondered what would happen to her if Dawson found out. I didn't want to betray her, not for anything.

"No," I whispered. "That's all there is."

He snuggled against me, his warm body lending me comfort and easing my mind. We stayed like that until he fell asleep, his arm tucked tightly around my waist as I lay cradled in his arms and thought about what to do.

I was here, with my clan and with Dawson, who made me believe he'd always be there for me if I'd let him. He'd stay by my side through it all, no questions asked.

And I wanted to let him. I *truly* did. I wanted to take a chance on love—to be a loyal member to my pack, embrace my new family, and finally, one day, possibly find my parents.

But as I lay there, drifting off to sleep, I knew no matter what Dawson offered me, whether it was safety, power, protection, or love, it would never be enough. There was a hole in my heart which could never be filled by him alone.

Before I settled into a deep sleep, my final thoughts were of the wolves I'd left behind.

And I knew what I had to do.

I'd been consumed by my desire for Dawson and my need to discover the truth about my past, but there was no denying that he wasn't the only man my soul craved.

The elder at Thunder Cove had told me the creatures from the shadow realm would never stop coming for me, which was why I'd left behind the three men who'd lit my heart on fire.

But as I snuggled in the arms of the Silver Creek Alpha and reveled in the intoxicating power flowing through my veins at having destroyed a wolf slayer, I knew what I had to do.

As soon as it was safe, I'd return to Grayson, Alex, and Cody, even for just one more chance to hold them in my arms and tell them how much they meant to me, how I could never—*would never*—forget them.

I'd been searching for my place in this strange, new world,

hoping to discover where I truly belonged. And while Silver Creek had welcomed me with open arms, the truth was, I'd already found my home, even if I couldn't be with them.

And home was where the heart was.

And my heart belonged to them.

CHAPTER SIXTEEN

CODY

I stood before the portal to Silver Creek, my heart aching for Ember, but my mind filled with so many questions and uncertainties.

"What if she doesn't want to come back?"

I turned, surprised to see Grayson making his way toward me, a defeated expression on his face as he vocalized the very thing that was weighing on my mind.

"Then we'll stand by her decision," I said. I'd been trying to steel myself for the reality that Ember may have found her clan and Silver Creek was everything she could want. If that were the case, I'd have to learn to live with it. But I needed to see for myself, to make sure she was okay.

"I'm not standing by *that* decision," Grayson replied, his eyes flashing. "*We* can protect her. She should've at least given us that chance."

A muscle flickered along his jaw as he clenched and unclenched it.

I didn't know what to say to him, especially with how much fire burned in his eyes. He was a temperamental Alpha with a heart of gold, and I knew now that he was coming to terms with how much Ember meant to him, he was blind to anything else. If she turned us away, I wasn't sure Grayson would recover.

Grayson crouched down and sifted through the white powder on the ground at our feet, his expression bleak.

"What the hell is this? It smells foul."

I'd noticed it earlier, but I'd been too caught up in looking for Ember to pay it too much attention. But now, as I studied it, something about the scent tugged at my memory. I squatted next to Grayson, taking a closer look at the glittery substance.

I inhaled sharply as an almost unfathomable idea came to mind.

"When we were kids..." I began, and out of the corner of my eye, I saw Grayson's head swivel toward me. "Dawson told us he had a way to stop people from tracking us when we wanted to explore other realms."

"Dawson was full of shit," Grayson replied tersely, but his features morphed from curious into confusion when I looked over at him.

"I'm not so sure about that." My chest tightened at the possibility Dawson had not only come for Ember but that he'd tried to prevent us from tracking her. "I think he was here. That he came for Ember."

"Son of a bitch," Grayson hissed, his face mottled with rage. He took a menacing step forward toward the portal. "If that's true, he'll pay for this."

Before I could reply, a voice rang out from behind us, "I'm coming with you!"

We turned to find Selena heading our way, a book clutched in her hand.

"No fucking way," Grayson replied, his jaw tightening yet again. "We aren't bringing her with us."

"Selena, what are you doing here?" I asked.

Her eyes brimmed with excitement as she opened the book

and held it out to us. "I found something. Something that could help Ember."

I glanced at Grayson, whose attention was centered on the page. "What exactly am I looking at, Selena?"

"Last night, Elgin brought me another book he found. It had this illustration of the eye of the moon." She pointed to the sketch on the page. "The text says whoever possesses the relic has power over the shadow realm."

I tried to speak, but no words came.

Selena continued, "But the piece was broken in half in an effort to keep the power from falling into the wrong hands."

"But you don't know where this relic is, much less both pieces," Grayson said bitterly. "How is this possibly going to help Ember?"

Selena's face screwed with annoyance, but she took a deep breath and schooled her features better than I would've had our places been reversed.

"I spent hours sifting through dozens of books. I tried to find *anything* I could about the shadow realm—anything that would give us some direction. *Any* lead is better than none."

"We don't have all the answers, Grayson," I said honestly. "But Selena's right, it's a start." I nodded in appreciation. "A great start. You did good finding this. But you need to stay here where it's safe. We don't know what we'll find when we enter Silver Creek."

I could see from the expression on her face that while she was disappointed, she knew what I said to be true. We couldn't go charging into another realm with a horde of people.

"Head back to the clan and wait for us, okay? I'll let you know as soon as we're back. I promise."

She nodded, tears glistening in her eyes. "Bring her home, Cody."

"Not without me."

I glanced over my shoulder. Alex was making his way toward us.

"We can't just leave the pack without an Alpha," Grayson replied, his amber eyes hard and serious. "You should stay behind."

"Not a chance. I'm coming with you." His tone left no room for debate. "I left Rylen in charge of managing the clan until we return. I don't expect we'll be gone long."

Grayson's brows lifted slightly as he assessed Alex. "Sounds like you have it all figured out. The man with the plan."

Alex shook his head at Grayson's snarky tone, and his gaze dipped downward. "I don't. But Ember needs us, and we're not going to let her down."

Alex reached out and placed a hand on Grayson's shoulder, squeezing gently for a moment, his eyes shadowed. "You were right. Ember deserves a man who'll be there for her, no matter what."

Grayson's chest rose as he took a deep breath. Then his gaze flicked to Alex, then me, as his lips lifted in a half-grin. "Well, apparently, she doesn't just have one man willing to go to the ends of the Earth for her," he replied. "She has three."

Tears, sudden and unexpected, pricked my eyes, but I blinked them away. I lifted my chin, determined to keep my cool, to be the backbone and strength my Alphas relied on, that Ember needed.

"Ready when you are, Alphas," I replied, holding Grayson's gaze.

"Let's go get our girl."

CHAPTER SEVENTEEN

EMBER

Dawson's lips brushed against my cheek as he whispered, "I'm heading out to speak to the clan about what had happened last night."

I tried to sit up in bed. "I'll…um…" I wanted to tell him I'd join him and help however I could. After all, it was my fault the monster had attacked the pack.

"You're so exhausted you can barely talk. You should just go back to bed," he insisted, gently pushing me back onto the mattress.

A few hours later, I woke up feeling as though I'd slept for days. My fingers reached for Dawson, but he still hadn't returned.

I slid out of bed and wrapped a sheet around me as I headed for the door. I wanted to get back to my room, get dressed, and then look for Dawson. I needed to be there for him, to help him explain to his clan all that had happened. They needed to know it wasn't their Alpha's fault.

"Ember, could I have a moment with you?"

I'd only taken a step out into the hallway when I saw Ciara, who stood a short distance away, a look of disbelief on her face.

"Of course," I replied, my face growing hot with embarrassment that she'd discovered me leaving her son's bedroom wrapped in nothing but his bedsheet.

Talk about a walk of shame.

I made a mental note to ask Dawson if this was a regular occurrence—his mother walking into his home unannounced. Though something about the way she lurked quietly at the end of the hallway told me it wasn't. I wondered if someone had told her about everything.

"I heard you spent the evening in Dawson's room," she continued, confirming my suspicions.

Well, lady, bring it on.

"I did."

She pursed her lips as though the thought of my being in such close proximity to her son disgusted her. She tried to mask her feelings with a nod of her head.

"Please join me in the library," she said. When I just stood there, looking like an idiot, she turned to me. "Please? It won't take long."

"Would you mind if I get dressed first? My room is just up the hall."

"Very well," she said. "I'll wait for you here."

I couldn't move fast enough as I scrambled off to my room. Once inside, I took a deep breath to steady myself and then threw on a t-shirt and jeans.

I loved being at Silver Creek, but the way Ciara looked at me with daggers in her eyes was becoming a problem I knew I had to address. I wanted her to accept me, so we could move past whatever *this* was.

I prayed her visit would be a short one.

As promised, she was waiting in the hallway. I followed her as she made her way down a staircase I hadn't seen before, then another.

I had no idea where the library was. But when we went

down another level, and we still hadn't reached the room, I got the notion she was steering me as far out of earshot as possible.

Finally, we reached the library, and the bookworm in me nearly lost her mind.

It was a large room, decorated in earthy tones, with floor-to-ceiling shelves filled with books on every wall except one, which boasted a massive stone fireplace. Several large, chocolate-brown sofas and chairs were scattered throughout the room, with a gorgeously plush loveseat tucked away in a reading nook.

If I weren't here, ready to have some nerve-wracking conversation with Dawson's mother, I would've been soaking it all in, smelling the leather-bound books, and reading as many as I could manage.

Instead, I took a seat across from Ciara and waited for her to speak.

"How are you doing?" she asked me.

Clearly, she wasn't here for small talk, nor did she likely even care about how I was doing. But I went along with it anyway, willing to play the game for as long as it took if it meant I could finally get to the bottom of why she didn't like me.

It stuck out to me that if she'd been told I'd spent the night with Dawson, then surely she'd heard about the lupus interfectorem and that I was the reason it had invaded the realm, yet she said nothing about it.

"I love being here," I replied truthfully. In turn, I asked Ciara about her trip to see her cousin. "Did you just get back? I thought you'd planned to be gone for a few days."

She peered at me, her eyes narrowing just slightly, and I got the feeling she was anxious to get right to the point but was trying to ease in slowly.

"I was supposed to be away longer, but I came rushing back when I heard about what happened yesterday. We're lucky no one got hurt…or killed."

There it was. The elephant in the room had finally been addressed.

"I know, and I'm so thankful for that. I feel sick about it all."

And that was the truth. I felt incredibly guilty, my heart heavy with the knowledge I'd be bringing danger with me wherever I went.

I was a dead woman walking.

"I can understand why since I've been informed you're the reason the creature entered our realm in the first place." Her stone-cold gaze was locked on my face, her emotions tucked away behind her steely facade, but I got the sense inside, she was raging. "Can you tell me how it came to be that you were marked?"

I took a deep breath and then gave her the rundown, skipping over the small details but telling her enough to where she understood I was in the human realm and a creature had attacked me from out of nowhere.

"So, you'd never encountered any magic or darkness before that night?"

"No," I replied. "Not ever. My life in the human world was pretty ordinary."

"I see," she murmured, thoughtfully. "And your wolf, it hadn't ever surfaced while you were in the human world?"

"No. She didn't emerge until the night of the Fallen Moon," I told her. "When I was in Thunder Cove."

I took a breath and hoped this line of questioning would quickly come to an end. The way she looked at me cut me like a knife, and even though I knew I shouldn't care, I did.

"I'm very sorry that happened to you."

But was she? Because the way she stared blankly at me told me otherwise. She seemed devoid of all emotion.

"And you don't know who your parents are?" she asked.

For some reason, that question struck my heart harder than any other. I was sure Ciara already knew that the identities of my parents remained a mystery. After all, I'd only just arrived, and no one had stepped forward to claim me.

"I don't." I shifted uncomfortably on the chair.

"Yet you felt drawn to this clan?"

I nodded. "When I met Dawson in the human world, we felt a connection. Then, when he came to Thunder Cove to meet me, it all made sense. As soon as I entered through the portal, my wolf felt at home."

"Dawson seems to have little doubt you belong here," she replied. "And I trust my son, though he's a little too much like his father." She shot me a sliver of a smile, but she looked at me like she was still trying to figure out whether to accept me or not.

"I believe this is my clan." I took a deep breath when my chest tightened with anxiety. This woman sure knew how to leave me feeling on edge. "I'm sure of it."

"Then your parents should be brave enough to come forward," she said softly. "They owe you an explanation, and they also owe the clan one." She lifted a hand as though she held the world in it. "Abandoning a shifter, even a half-one, in the human world is an unforgivable offense."

"What would happen?" I asked, the words tumbling from my lips before I could think about whether it was the kind of question I should be asking Ciara. "If they stepped forward…would they be imprisoned?"

Ciara crossed her arms and quirked her eyebrows. "What do *you* think should happen to them? These people left you for dead. Surely, you want them to pay for such cruelty."

I caught my breath and stiffened at the question I wasn't sure how to answer.

"I don't know," I replied honestly. "Perhaps there's a reason why my parents left me in the human world."

It wasn't the first time I'd thought of the possibility, though I'd been angry for so long I never let the thought fully form. It was like I was giving them an excuse. But at the same time, part of my heart wanted to believe there had to be some sort of explanation.

Ciara studied me with a veiled look, then swallowed hard and flicked her hand toward a bookshelf. "There are countless tomes which speak of the importance of clan loyalty, of keeping our pack strong. Every wolf knows how important it is to find a full-blooded mate to ensure our future, our survival. The fact that one of your parents is a shifter and mated with a human is *not* acceptable."

I stared at her, speechless. She knew I was only a halfling and her words were beyond cruel. She was telling me my heritage went against nature, against what the pack stood for.

Rage bristled through me, but I swallowed it down, knowing Ciara would get a kick out of seeing my emotions. I refused to let this woman know how much she affected me.

"I can't help the fact I am half-human," I replied stiffly. "And I won't apologize for it. Perhaps my parents fell in love, and—"

"In love?" She chuckled darkly as though the idea that my parents may have spat in the face of such archaic laws to follow their hearts was more than absurd. "Yet they couldn't love you? They left you on the steps of a nunnery. That is *not* love."

"How did you know they left me with the nuns? I never told you…"

It was clear Ciara had realized one second too late she'd said something she shouldn't have. She quickly stood up, making herself busy by pouring herself a glass of water from a nearby jug.

"Ciara?" I hardly dared take a breath as she stood with her back to me. "Do you know something you haven't shared with me?"

A million questions bounced around my head, incoherent and fast, but they all came to a screeching halt when she turned to me, her mouth twisted with annoyance, her eyes never leaving mine. They appeared to be almost black, no longer arctic blue—though they were equally unnerving.

"As you might imagine, I've had eyes on you since you arrived. As the Alpha's mother, it's my job to help protect our clan," Ciara muttered. "Dawson had assigned a small team to research…to try and figure out who your parents are."

I straightened, the news causing a spike of adrenaline to race through my body.

"And what did they uncover?"

Ciara exhaled deeply, and I caught her shrug. "All in good time. We don't have answers just yet."

My heart sank the more she talked, but I nodded, trying not to let my disappointment show.

"Oh, save the waterworks," she snapped, spotting the tears before I felt them. "Now that we have a witness in custody, we'll have answers soon enough."

"A witness?" I asked, my brows knitted. "Who? Tell me."

She looked at me expectantly, and I choked out the word as though it burned me, which made her snicker.

"Please."

In a heartbeat, Ciara's victorious smirk fell, and in its place was…contempt.

"She's a witch amongst wolves," she hissed. "Dark magic hiding in plain sight. We found letters in her room…letters which speak of her bringing a child from our realm into the human world." Her hand curled into a tight fist. "And you'll be happy to know we found your necklace in her room as well. I'll see that it's promptly returned to you."

An invisible fist clamped down around my heart, and my mind became a blur.

"Ravena," I choked.

The witch with the gentle eyes had used magic to help me fight off the shadow beast's hold. Had it not been for her, I never would've survived.

"She took me to the human world?"

"Yes," Ciara replied. "After all the clan has done for her, taking her in when she had nowhere else to go, yet she betrayed us. She betrayed you."

"But that can't be," I muttered, trying to make sense of what Ciara was telling me. "She helped me—"

"A witch like Ravena doesn't help *anyone* but herself," Ciara said sharply. "You shouldn't trust anything she may have told you." Her lips spread into a twisted smile, making my insides turn. "But you needn't worry about her now. She's at the Hall of Justice. Soon she'll be exiled for the traitor she is."

"Hall of Justice? What are you doing to her?"

Ciara glanced at the tiny watch on her wrist and ignored me. "Dawson should be arriving there shortly, now that he's been informed of the situation. Once our men get through with Ravena, she'll never be able to hurt anyone again."

A blend of a gasp and a sob slipped out of me, but before I could utter another word, Ciara headed toward the door, pausing only long enough to glance back at me briefly, and then she was gone.

I tried to make sense of everything I'd learned as both fear and hope blossomed in my chest.

Fear for Ravena and for whatever fate awaited her for her role in taking me from my clan.

And hope that she might hold the key to unlocking the secrets of my past.

Ciara said she was being held prisoner in a Hall of Justice. I knew that if I wanted to finally get answers, that was where I needed to go.

CHAPTER EIGHTEEN

EMBER

I raced out of Dawson's castle and into the bright afternoon sun. I wasn't sure where the Hall of Justice was located, so I headed aimlessly down a nearby street, looking for road signs to guide me.

Ciara had mentioned she had spies, eyes on me, which meant anyone I might ask for directions could very well run and tell her I was looking for Ravena.

But, as I made my way down one gray cobblestone path to another which split off in four directions—with no street signs to be found—it quickly became apparent if I didn't ask someone for help, I'd never reach my destination.

I turned when I heard a horse-drawn carriage behind me and quickly stepped to the side to allow it to pass.

"Excuse me!" I called out to the man in it, and to my relief, he yanked on the reins and stopped just ahead of where I stood. "Can you help me?"

"I can try," he replied with a curious smile. "What do you need?"

"I haven't been in this realm for very long," I began, praying I sounded calmer than I felt. "And I'm interested in learning everything I can about the clan. I thought I'd start by visiting the Hall of Justice. Can you tell me where to find it?"

The man pursed his lips, his eyes glued to my face.

"I'm not so sure that's a good place to start learning about our history," he said thoughtfully. "Perhaps the library would be better? We have lots of wonderful books about our clan"

I smiled, trying my best to act casual. "That's a great idea, but I'd love to see the Hall of Justice as well. If you wouldn't mind pointing me in the right direction, I'd appreciate it."

"I can do better than that. Hop on." He lifted the reins as he waited for me to climb onto the carriage. "It's on my way. I'll drop you off. I'm Lawrence, by the way."

"I'm Ember."

The idea of hitching a ride with a stranger, even in an open carriage, gave me pause. Still, the warmth in the man's smile convinced me it was safe. A few seconds later, I climbed up beside him.

It dawned on me—not for the first time—just how different Silver Creek was from Thunder Cove. In this realm, it was as though time stood still. Things moved slower here—everything but my heart which beat wildly at the thought of learning about my past.

"The Hall of Justice isn't that far away," Lawrence told me. "But it's on the other side of the creek. The ride can get a little bumpy, so hold on tight."

I hadn't traveled this way before, so when Lawrence gently tapped the reins to get the horse into a steady trot, it took me a few minutes to get used to the wobbly movement of the carriage.

He chuckled. "Don't worry. We won't tip over."

I gave him a grateful smile for his reassurance.

"You're the halfling," he said, though there was no malice in his tone, only interest. "I bet you're happy to be home finally."

"I am," I agreed. "Silver Creek is a beautiful place."

He made small talk as other carriages, as well as bicycles, passed by. It didn't take long before the smells and scenery changed, though the view ahead was just as picturesque.

I swallowed a breath of the briny air drifting in from the nearby bay. When I looked back, I saw we'd already covered a lot of distance as the gleam of castles disappeared.

"There," Lawrence said as we made our way around another bend. He pointed toward a building, then brought the carriage to an abrupt halt. "The Hall of Justice is the big, gray building on the right."

The Hall of Justice was an imposing structure which spanned three stories, with large, stone pillars supporting the massive building and a stunning clock tower overhead.

I thanked him as I eased down from the seat. He waved at me in return before jiggling the reins, making the horse take off.

Now that I was here, I realized getting to the location was the easy part. Figuring out how to get *into* the Hall of Justice and find Ravena was a whole other story. I peered around, trying to decide whether to walk straight through the front door or find a side entrance and sneak in unnoticed.

I watched the people making their way in and out of the building, all of them dressed in smart-looking, business suits. I couldn't help but acknowledge my casual outfit would likely pose a problem at my attempt to appear incognito. I certainly didn't look like I belonged there.

Suddenly, I felt so ridiculous. I had no plan—*as usual*—just sheer determination and an overwhelming desire to finally uncover the truth.

As I got closer to the building, I breathed a sigh of relief when I spotted Dawson making his way toward the building's entrance. I was about to call out to him when he turned as though he sensed me behind him, a short distance away.

I prayed he wouldn't turn me away or refuse to let me speak

to Ravena on my own. No matter what she might say, I needed to know the truth. But as I picked up my pace, a voice captured my attention.

"Ember!"

I heard my name, the familiar voice reaching deep into my soul, compelling me to turn toward it.

"Grayson..."

When my gaze met his, my heart soared, and the air leeched from my lips as though I could finally breathe with ease.

He was here, in Silver Creek, just a few feet away, close enough I could take a few steps and touch his handsome face.

"Ember...you're okay." His voice seemed strained, as though he was struggling to believe I was standing in front of him.

I blinked back tears, overcome with shame for having left without saying goodbye.

How could I have been so heartless?

It had only been a few days, but Grayson looked different somehow, as though he'd let go of some of the rigid control he always seemed to wear like armor. When Dawson appeared at my side, Grayson's expression clouded over, and the moment of softness was gone.

"I'm happy to see you're alive and well." Grayson's eyes were once again locked on mine, and even when Dawson squeezed my shoulder protectively, Grayson refused to acknowledge him.

"I'm so sorry. I—"

"That's all I needed to know," he said, interrupting my apology, his tone as cold as the northern winds. "I just wanted to make sure you were safe. Cody and Alex were worried about you."

I turned to Dawson, hoping he'd recognize I needed a moment alone with Grayson, but he didn't budge. Instead, he looked at Grayson as though he too had so much he needed to say but was holding back. Finally, Dawson took a step forward.

"Welcome back to Silver Creek, Grayson. It's been a long time. Too long."

"You know damn well I never wanted to step foot inside this realm again," Grayson growled, his nostrils flaring.

I thought back to what Cody had told me about Grayson having history with Silver Creek. And even though I didn't know what had happened, it was clear there was bad blood between them as they stood face to face like two wild animals staring each other down.

Grayson nodded toward me. "I just came to see if Ember was here. She left without saying a word."

"You're a good man," Dawson told him. "But she's in good hands. She's with her clan."

I didn't miss the way Grayson suddenly avoided looking at me, and while I understood why, I couldn't control the grief which ravaged my heart.

"Dawson, can you give us a minute?" I asked after the silence had dragged on for what felt like hours.

Dawson's brow furrowed at my words, and for a moment, I thought he'd refuse, but to my relief, he took a step back.

"I need to talk to you as soon as you're finished here," he told me. "It's important."

I knew he was about to tell me they had Ravena in custody—that today could be the day I finally unlocked the secrets to my past.

But as I stood in front of Grayson, his gorgeous features strained by a pained expression, I knew he deserved answers before I got mine.

"I know. I hope Ravena will open up to me."

Dawson cocked an eyebrow in surprise at my response, but I didn't explain how I knew.

"I'll meet you inside after I speak with Grayson."

Dawson nodded slowly, but he didn't say another word to me. Instead, he focused his attention on Grayson, who waited, arms crossed, his jaw tightening. "I'd like to speak with you before you head back to Thunder Cove."

Grayson narrowed his gaze; his brow drew tight into a frown. "We don't have anything to talk about."

"We do," Dawson replied sharply. "And you know it. It's been so long, Grayson. Just give me a chance to explain. That's all I ask."

Dawson didn't wait for a response—and it was clear he wouldn't have gotten one.

Grayson watched him walk away, and even when I deliberately stepped into his line of sight, he turned his head, directing his attention to something off in the distance.

"Please, Grayson, talk to me."

He bit his bottom lip as though he didn't trust himself not to say things he might regret. Then his eyes met mine once again, and he shrugged, a gentle lifting of his shoulders which only emphasized all that hard muscle.

"What do you expect me to say, Ember? You left us without a word. You didn't even say goodbye." Anguish threaded his voice.

"I know," I replied. "And I'm sorry. I truly am. If I could go back—"

"You *can't* go back," he growled, cutting me off. His gaze tore from mine once again, moving to where Dawson once stood, and his golden eyes darkened. "None of us can. What's done is done."

It was clear he wasn't just referring to the fact I'd left without saying goodbye. The way he clenched his jaw told me whatever was bothering him had just as much to do with Dawson as it did with me.

"Grayson, I never meant to hurt you." I longed to reach for him, but I wasn't sure it would be welcome.

He studied me a moment, then smirked. "You *didn't* hurt me. But we put our clan at risk for you. The least you could've done was tell us you were leaving." His tone was brittle, detached. "I came here to make sure you weren't causing problems for someone else. I wouldn't want Thunder Cove blamed for having brought you into this world."

"So, that's it?" I countered. "You're just here to make sure I'm not a problem for this clan like I was for yours?"

"That's *not* what I said, and you fucking know it," he bit back. "Don't play games with me, Ember. You left. Your wolf awakened, and you couldn't get away from us fast enough. And this…" He spread his arms out. "This is where you chose to run off to? Silver Creek?"

My gaze dropped to my feet, as did my heart. The anger in Grayson's tone was justified, I knew it. But it didn't make the pain slicing across my chest any easier to bear.

"This is my clan, Grayson." When my eyes dared to meet his once again, I saw a wickedness in his expression that startled me. "I had to know where I came from. And now I do."

He shook his head and scoffed. "Silver Creek is your clan. Of course, it is." He stared at me as if he was waiting for me to take it all back, but I couldn't. It was the truth, and he deserved nothing but honesty.

"What can I do?" I pleaded with him, trying to keep my voice from breaking. "What can I do to make things right?"

Grayson studied me a moment, his expression revealing nothing. Then, after a long moment, he sighed, raking his fingers through his short, dark hair.

"There's nothing to do. You've found your clan, discovered where you belong. No one can fault you for that. We're wolves…you would've never been happy until you'd met your clan." The sincerity in his voice flooded my heart with emotion. "That's all I ever wanted for you, you know. For you to be happy."

I bit back a sob, my teeth resting on my lower lip as I tried not to fall to pieces.

I wanted to tell him that while Silver Creek was my clan and birthplace, I wasn't so sure it was where I belonged. I was here to find answers—answers which could be just a few feet away—but my heart hadn't left Thunder Cove...hadn't left him.

But I also didn't want to complicate things for Grayson, Alex, or Cody.

As I stood so close to him, my soul longed to touch him, a tide of desire quickly weakening my resolve and threatening to sweep me away. It made all my reasons for leaving seem absurd, but the truth was, my situation hadn't changed. I had to find a way to release the shadow realm's hold on me before I could ever be free to love—to live.

Otherwise, I'd only put the people I cared for in danger.

It dawned on me, not for the first time, that just by coming to Silver Creek, Grayson had unknowingly put himself in harm's way.

"A creature attacked last night," I told him.

He stiffened, his eyes filling with concern.

"Are you okay?" Grayson's voice dropped to an almost whisper as his eyes swept over my body as though he was looking for any signs I'd been injured in the attack.

"I'm fine," I reassured him. "But you shouldn't be here. I'm marked, Grayson. Which means the shadow realm will keep sending creatures until they've destroyed me."

"I know," Grayson replied. "Selena told us." He paused. "I just wish you had told us yourself."

I pulled my gaze from him, ashamed I hadn't turned to them, hadn't shared with them everything I'd discovered.

"Look at me."

Like a coward, I paused, but then he dipped his head, forcing me to stare at him.

"You did what you thought was best," he told me. "It's your life on the line, not ours. But, Ember, you shouldn't have to battle a monster on your own."

I drew in a few deep breaths. "Dawson and his men helped

me destroy it," I told him. "I don't think I could've done it on my own. I'm not that strong yet."

At the mention of Dawson's name, Grayson's eyes filled with torment, though he nodded his approval. "A wolf's pack should always stand next to their own, no matter what. I'm glad Silver Creek is doing that."

"Thunder Cove means just as much to me," I countered in a shaky voice. "It'll always hold a special place in my heart. My wolf surfaced there."

"She did," Grayson replied. "And she's beautiful. You both are."

The intensity of his gaze washed over me as he moved a step closer, the heat from his body singeing across my skin.

His lips fought a smile. "But you're so much more than that."

I was desperate for him to touch me, but I could tell there was a war going on in his mind. His lips finally curved into a smile.

"I've missed you," I told him, hoping he could hear the sincerity in my voice. I needed him to know despite finding my clan, I hadn't forgotten him. "I've missed you all so much."

Grayson exhaled a heavy sigh, and some of his guard lowered. "I've missed you, too. I couldn't stop thinking about you." Fire flashed in those wickedly golden eyes, and the heat of his unflinching stare crashed over me in one long, lapping wave. "And I wasn't the only one."

I opened my mouth to ask him how Alex and Cody were doing, but before I could form the words, Grayson's lips curved into a crooked smile, and it made my heart flutter like a bird's wings against my rib cage.

"They're here…in Silver Creek," he informed me. "They needed to see you just as much as I did."

Emotion overwhelmed me at the thought of seeing Alex and Cody again. Suddenly, they stepped into view, and a blend of a gasp and a sob slipped out of me.

Grayson caught the expression on my face and peered behind him as Cody and Alex seemed to notice us at the same time, their pace quickening to a jog.

"Ember!" Alex called out to me.

As I took a step forward, wanting to run to him, Grayson grabbed my wrist. I turned back, my eyes searching his face. This time all I saw was desire as he tugged me toward him.

"I don't want to be away from you again," he told me, his voice a low rumble.

I lost myself in Grayson's strong embrace, his arms banding around me, holding me tight against his chest. He smelled like the fresh ocean breeze of Thunder Cove, and I nearly wept at the memory of strolling with him on the boardwalk when he'd first opened up to me and told me about his mother and their shared love of painting.

"I'm so sorry," I wept against his chest, but he didn't say a word or let go.

His arms only tightened around me, one hand reaching up to hold the back of my head, his fingers tangling into my hair.

"I'm so very—"

"I know," he whispered into my hair. "You had to find your family...your clan. You have nothing to be sorry for."

But he was wrong. I had so many things to be sorry for, but as he cradled me in his arms, my heart found shelter from the deep sadness I'd felt since leaving them.

"Ember, oh my God, I'm so happy you're okay." It was Alex's voice that reached out to me as Grayson reluctantly released me. "We were so worried."

"I know," I said, my voice cracking. "I'm sorry I left the way I did."

"That doesn't matter," Alex replied softly as he hugged me. "You're okay, and that's all that matters."

I wound my arms around his neck, and when he lowered his face to rest against my cheek, I peeked over his shoulder at

Cody, who stood a few feet away. He wore an expression I couldn't read. His shoulders rose as he took a deep breath and then let it slowly escape his lips.

"I will never forgive myself for leaving as I did," I told Alex.

His hands smoothed along my back before they rested at my waist. He didn't hold me as long as Grayson had, but when he backed up and peered down at me, the glimmer in his eyes told me he forgave me.

I eased back, my hand sweeping down Alex's arm as I turned toward Cody, who was still standing a short distance away.

He didn't move when I turned to him, didn't close the distance between, or take me into his arms like my heart desperately wished he would. I could barely breathe. Every muscle in my body tensed as he held my gaze as though he was punishing me.

I deserved this. I deserved to feel his wrath.

Then something in his expression broke, the hardness melting ever-so-slightly, replaced by what looked like relief.

I took a tentative step forward, as though testing it out, afraid he'd turn from me.

"Cody…" I shuffled ahead slightly, more determined this time, slowly erasing the space.

When he finally shifted in my direction, I nearly cried out, my heart aching to be in his arms.

"I'm sorry. I shouldn't have left that way," I prattled, my apology a mere whisper, lost in the heat of his stare. More words, broken but necessary, as my heart did the talking, and when I continued to blurt out just how much I'd missed him, he hushed me with a finger pressed to my lips.

His touch, ever so light, heated my body. My knees grew so weak I nearly collapsed. Then I was in his arms, my ramblings muffled against his chest as tears streaked down my cheeks.

Cody didn't let go, not even when I'd soaked the front of his shirt and buried my face into his chest. I closed my eyes, every inch of my body thrumming with desire, but it was more than that—much more.

"You didn't deserve to be treated like that," I told him, choking out the words as he continued clutching me against his chest. "You've been so good to me...so kind."

Cody took a deep breath, his shoulders tensing, and then he tipped my chin up, so my eyes met his. My breath caught in my throat when he gave me an easy grin, the anger in his gaze replaced by something else.

"Don't ever do that again," he murmured, so low the words washed over me like a warm caress. "Don't you ever leave me like that."

I nodded wordlessly, my gaze lingering on his lips. I wished I could kiss his hurt away.

Cody studied me as though he was searching for answers I hadn't given, like he needed to be sure I understood the pain I'd caused. I breathed him in, wishing I hadn't been so foolish, so cruel.

Finally, he seemed to sense my feelings, how deeply sorry I was for hurting him. Then I was rewarded by the softness of his lips as he dipped his head to kiss my cheek, then lower along my jaw, before teasing his mouth down the curve of my neck.

My lips burned to feel his, but instead, he swept his mouth over my chin, pressing a soft kiss there, just inches from where I wanted him, before lifting his head, a faint smile crossing his lips.

He knew I'd received his message loud and clear. If I ran from him again, I'd never feel his lips on mine or his hands on my curves.

"You don't have to stay away," Alex said when Cody stepped back, releasing me. "Silver Creek is your clan, but you'll always be welcome at Thunder Cove. There's no reason you can't spend time in both realms."

His words brought tears to my eyes. These three men only

wanted to protect me, care for me, safeguard me against the danger which would come for me again and again.

Suddenly, I remembered Ravena being held inside the Hall of Justice, and I practically sputtered my words, trying to catch Grayson, Alex, and Cody up to speed.

"So, do you think she knows who your parents are?" Alex asked me.

"I don't know, but I need to find out. Ravena helped me face the beast. If she took me from this realm, she must have had a good reason."

Cody nodded slowly as he considered everything I'd told them. "Hopefully, she'll tell you everything she knows." His eyes darkened slightly. "Unless she's being threatened and is too afraid to."

"It's Silver Creek," Grayson added sharply. "Of course, she's being threatened. Someone likely forced her to take Ember into the human world. It'll take a lot of work to get her to crack if she thinks she'll be punished."

"How would she be punished?" I asked fearfully. I wasn't familiar with how a pack might reprimand one of its members, but I couldn't stand the thought of Ravena being hurt in any way.

"Depends on the crime," Cody replied. Then he peered at Grayson out of the corner of his eye. "And the clan."

Something in the way he said that made me feel like Silver Creek was known for dealing out harsher punishments than Thunder Cove. My breath hitched in my throat. We needed to get to Ravena now.

"Offer her sanctuary," Alex said in that smooth voice of his, his expression somber. "If Silver Creek is threatening banishment, and Ravena has a good reason for taking Ember into the human world, we should offer her a home at Thunder Cove. No one should be afraid to speak the truth."

Cody nodded, and to my surprise, so did Grayson, though his eyes held a hint of doubt about Ravena's innocence.

"Let's go find out." Cody stepped toward the Hall of Justice as Dawson met us outside the entrance.

He smiled at Cody and Alex, clearly happy to see them. Then his attention returned to me, and I saw he wore a look of understanding.

I'd told him something I hadn't told anyone else, that I loved Grayson, Alex, and Cody. And when Grayson reached out and took my hand in his, though Dawson flinched, the knowing expression never left his face.

I promised myself that once I had the answers I'd been searching for, despite whatever came next, I would finally tell them all what my heart had always known.

CHAPTER NINETEEN

EMBER

We made our way into the Hall of Justice and then followed Dawson down a flight of stairs into a shadowy basement. A few minutes later, he unlocked a door which opened into an interrogation room. Ravena was shackled to a desk. Her head hung low, and her shoulders sagged as though she carried the weight of the world on them.

My heart ached at the sight of her. Ravena's face was pale as she wiped her cheeks, collecting fallen tears with a sniffle. She looked like she'd aged a hundred years. When she heard the door clicking and peered up at us, her eyes widened in fear.

"We're not going to hurt you, Ravena," Dawson reassured her. "We just need answers."

Dawson slid out a chair for me, and I sat across from her while Grayson took a seat next to me. When I peeked over my shoulder, I found Cody and Alex waited by the door as though they sensed how afraid Ravena was and knew being surrounded by four men wouldn't help the situation.

"You helped me fight the lupus interfectorem…" I bit my lip, carefully considering my words. I needed her to understand I'd do all that I could to protect her from whatever consequences might befall her, no matter what. "With the potion, but also with the gargoyle. I know you're a good person, Ravena. I need you to tell me the truth."

She took a deep breath but said nothing as she studied my face.

"Ravena, we need you to start talking." Grayson reached over and wrapped his fingers around mine. "Ember deserves to know why you took her from this world into the human one."

"You must have had your reasons," I reasoned, softening my tone to sway her to start talking. "Please tell me who my parents are and why you carried me into the human world."

"You left her for dead," Dawson added angrily from beside me. "Ember is lucky to be alive. And she deserves an explanation. *Now.*"

Ravena's attention suddenly anchored on Dawson, and she visibly stiffened. "I did *not* leave her for dead," she replied rigidly. "Ember is alive only because I brought her into the human world. Had she stayed here..." Her voice faded as she caught her breath.

"What would've happened?" I asked her.

I felt we were on the cusp of convincing her to tell us all she knew, but when she lowered her gaze again, I was terrified she'd once again retreated into silence.

"Please, Ravena. Nothing will happen to you. I promise." My tone was filled with desperation as I begged her to speak.

"My child," she replied. "Sadly, that's not your decision. I'll be banished from Silver Creek." When her gaze met mine, the fear had faded a bit and was replaced by something much more complex.

I peered at Dawson, unsure what she was talking about. I wished he'd reassure Ravena she could stay, that she only had to tell the truth, and then everything would work itself out. But to my surprise, he firmed his jaw and nodded coldly.

"You're a pretender who came here under false pretenses.

You were welcomed into Silver Creek many years ago because the Alpha believed you needed help. Yet you never told anyone you are a witch?"

"I'm a *halfling*," Ravena said sharply. "Just like Ember and so many others who are forced to turn their backs on who they are. I had a home, a coven that meant the world to me." Tears welled in her eyes at the mention of it. "Yet I was punished, exiled by them when I used my magic outside of my realm."

"There are reasons such rules exist," Dawson countered, his anger unwavering. "Magic is dangerous and unpredictable. We are wolves, *not* supernaturals. We need our clan to always feel safe. You should've been honest when you came here all those years ago."

"I *was* honest," Ravena said, her voice barely above a whisper. "And I had no choice but to come here and sell my magic. There were few of us left in my coven after the vampires invaded our realm and savagely killed my family. We had nothing of value left but our magic."

"Why did you choose to come to Silver Creek?" I asked, sensing there was far more to the story than Ravena simply seeking refuge in this realm.

"There were people here who offered to pay for my services, and my sister's. We sent the gold coins we earned back to our coven in the hope of saving them, of being able to rebuild all we'd lost. It was harmless magic at first. A love potion, a spell to appear youthful. Then things changed."

I straightened my shoulders. "Changed how?"

"Some people craved things only dark magic could bring," Ravena replied, her voice low. "I refused their demands, but my sister was weak, tempted by the offer of greater gold, by her thirst for power."

"No one from this clan would dare bring a witch here." Dawson scowled.

It was clear he was unwilling to accept what Ravena was

saying—that people in his pack had invited her here in exchange for her magic.

"And if someone did, you need to tell us who."

I watched helplessly as any headway we'd made vanished. Ravena retreated, her frail body seeming to shrink under Dawson's furious gaze, and she looked away.

We needed to tread lightly, and Dawson was doing a terrible job at it.

"Can you tell me who my parents are?" I asked, redirecting the conversation. I knew Dawson wouldn't stop berating Ravena until she revealed who'd brought her into his realm, but I needed to get answers about my past. "I've spent my entire life wondering about them, wishing I knew why they'd abandoned me."

Ravena shook her head, her eyes filled with sadness and truth. "Your parents didn't abandon you, Ember. They would've never done that."

"Then please tell me. Who are they?"

"Your mother, Ivy, was a beautiful human with such a joyful spirit," she told me. "She was so young and innocent. She didn't know what would happen just because she fell in love with a shifter." Ravena paused, and for a second, I was fearful she'd clam up again, but instead, she stretched her hands across the table, the shackles biting into her wrists as she reached as far as she could. I leaned forward and let her take my hands in hers.

"Your father loved your mother very much. He would've gone to the ends of the world just to see her smile. And he would've given up *anything* to be with her. He couldn't possibly know what was going to happen."

She paused briefly, and I only dared to nod, barely breathing, not wanting to miss a word.

"Your father is a good man, a true hero. And he loved his clan dearly." She peered up at Dawson, her gaze hardening. "But he wasn't afraid to embrace others, no matter where they came from or who they were. Even halflings like us…"

My chest had swelled with pride at the thought of my father being a good man. "Where are my parents now?" I thought back to the night when Ravena took me to her cottage. She'd told me my parents weren't here, that they weren't even in this realm. "Are they alive?"

A pained expression crossed Ravena's face, and she squeezed my fingers a little tighter. "Your father used to venture into the human realm quite often, mainly because he was curious about humans. He wanted to understand them, to learn all he could so maybe one day our kind wouldn't be so feared. He dreamed of a world where humans and shifters could coexist. And on one of his travels, he met your mother."

Beside me, Grayson shifted as he crossed his arms over his chest. When I peered at him, his features were strained—his jaw tense, his eyes filled with sadness—but he remained silent.

"Your mother was so excited when she found out she was pregnant with you. She started sewing baby clothes right away, in all the colors and styles." She smiled, though it never reached her eyes. "Even your name was chosen long before you were born."

Her voice took on a gentle, whimsical tone as she allowed herself to get lost in her memories. "Your mother told me there could be no other name for her first baby girl. That you were the light of her life, the spark of hope for a better future she'd been longing for. She would've been so proud of the woman you've become."

Tears welled in my eyes when I realized she'd been referring to my mother in the past tense.

"My mother is dead." It wasn't a question.

I took a deep breath, willing the swirling sick feeling in my gut to fade. Somehow I knew it to be true even before Ravena tipped her head and gently nodded.

"How did she die?"

Ravena's lips twitched as though she was trying to find a way to tell me that wouldn't shatter my soul, and this time I was the one who squeezed her hand. "It's okay. You can tell me."

"We didn't know that a human couldn't survive the birth of a shifter," she began. "The farther she got into her pregnancy, the weaker she became. So very weak. Your father somehow managed to bring her into this realm, despite the fact she was human. He hoped it would give her strength, hoping she might survive, but it was too late."

I pushed my chair back and leaned forward, my elbows resting on my knees, the world stuttering into slow motion as my stomach heaved, hit with another wave of nausea.

Breathe, Ember. Just breathe.

My mother hadn't abandoned me. She'd lost her life bringing me into this world.

"And what happened to my father?" I asked between breaths, my voice cracking.

The room had gone deathly silent, no one daring to interrupt our conversation. Grayson's hand slid over my back, stroking me lovingly, letting me know he was there for me.

"Your father is the one who welcomed me into this realm...*his* realm," Ravena told me, her expression revealing just how much she cared for him. "He was so kind to me. He was kind to everyone in his clan." She glanced at Dawson as if she wanted to remind him of what being a leader meant.

"My father was the Alpha of this clan," I gasped, finally reading between the lines of what she'd said. Frantically, I peered at Dawson, cocking a brow in question.

"Don't worry. We aren't related," he assured me, giving my shoulder a squeeze and eliciting a low growl from Grayson.

Ravena nodded. "But he was taken from his realm while he was grieving the loss of your mother. Taken by dark magic."

"Did you have anything to do with that?" I asked her, praying she hadn't.

"I would *never* have betrayed your father," she answered firmly, and I believed her. "Silver Creek took in my sister and me when we had nowhere to go. I thought she was as loyal as I was. But she saw an opportunity to rise to power. To take control of this clan."

She sucked in another breath, letting the air slowly escape her lips. "My sister is lost to me now. Her heart is as black as night. The only reason she had allowed me to stay here was that I kept her secret. Even now, she'd never expect me to reveal it. But you deserve to know the truth. I wanted to tell you the moment I discovered you were here, in this realm, but I was too afraid."

"I understand," I told her. And I did. I saw the sorrow in her face and heard the deep sadness in every word she spoke. And above all, the truth rang out.

"I tried to be there for your father when he lost your mother, but he was so broken." Ravena swallowed down her tears. "He hid away from the world, refusing to speak to anyone, but I heard whispers. People wanted to uproot him, replace him."

My chest tightened. "Replace him? How?"

"Tread carefully," Dawson warned Ravena, his voice low as he got up to pace the floor behind me. "What you're saying is treasonous. You'd do well to watch your tongue."

My gaze darted around, trying to understand what was happening as the tension in the room grew even more unbearable.

"What secret did you keep?" Cody asked. It was the first time he'd spoken since we'd entered the room. "What did your sister do, Ravena?"

Ravena's gaze clicked over to Cody as though she'd just realized there were other people in the room. Then she peered over to Alex. A hint of a smile graced her lips as though she recognized the gentleness of his spirit, but it quickly faded.

"My sister called the darkness to claim our Alpha and those who he loved most. No one in your father's lineage was to survive. That way there could never be a question about who would replace him." Ravena drew a ragged breath. "Your father was too caught up in his sorrow to fight the beast, so it took him. The clan simply thought he'd left, blamed his broken heart on him abandoning them, but that isn't the truth. He would've never walked away from his people...from you." Ravena's eyes shifted to me, her attention fully anchored on my face. "I brought you from this realm into the human one before the beast could mark you too. I prayed your wolf wouldn't surface in the human world and you could grow up happy without danger at your heels."

"A lupus interfectorem can only claim the soul of a wolf," I murmured as I took in everything I'd learned from Ravena, as well as what the Thunder Cove elder had told me. "Until my wolf surfaced, I was safe. You did the only thing you could do."

Ravena nodded weakly. "Your wolf would've emerged long ago if you'd stayed in this realm. But in the human world, I hoped she would stay dormant. I thought you'd be safe."

"You saved my life, Ravena. You took me away because you knew it was the only chance I had."

"Had your father's heart not been so broken, he would've been strong enough to destroy the beast, to save you. He was a brave man, a fearless warrior. But my sister and her lover used his grief against him. His heart was too broken, his sadness too great. He didn't see the monster coming. I only wish I could've warned him, but it was too late."

"How would your sister and her lover have gained power by destroying the Alpha?" Grayson asked her. "Only the next in the bloodline would be made Alpha." Suddenly, his gaze darkened as though he'd uncovered something. "Or a beta."

Ravena's gaze shifted to Dawson, and I followed it. He appeared distraught, his brow furrowed, his arms crossed over his chest.

"My sister positioned herself to be with the next Alpha," Ravena continued when Dawson remained silent, a grave expression on his face. "Ember, when the beast took your father, the role of Alpha went to the man closest to him."

This time Dawson had a visceral reaction. He clenched his fists, his eyes widening with understanding before they sparked with rage. "No," he whispered. "No...he couldn't have." A breath later, his posture changed, and his shoulders sagged.

"Dawson, what is it?" I asked, not understanding what any of this meant.

He pinned his gaze on me, his stormy eyes pleading for me to understand what he was about to say. "When my father was dying, he told me that he'd betrayed his Alpha, though he didn't tell me how exactly," Dawson explained, his voice soft and threaded with sadness, "He'd carried the guilt around for years, but only in his final moments did he confess."

"I still don't understand what this has to do with my parents," I answered, frustrated that I seemed to be the only one in the room who didn't understand the gravity of what Ravena had revealed. "Or with me."

"Dawson's father betrayed yours," Grayson explained, his voice steadier than my ragged breathing, though it was corded with sadness. He wrapped his arm around me protectively as my gaze flew to Dawson, who nodded slowly, grief clouding his handsome features.

"Ravena's sister is Ciara," he admitted, his voice nearly breaking. "My mother."

CHAPTER TWENTY

DAWSON

Rage burned through my veins like hot lava wanting to be set loose to destroy those who'd hurt me and the woman I'd vowed to protect.

I could barely control my wolf who growled with the need to surface. He wanted to attack, to defend what he felt was ours.

My parents had conspired to destroy the former Alpha, Ember's father, so my father could claim the role with my mother by his side.

My mother was a halfling, a mix of witch and wolf. *Did that mean I was too?* I'd never felt the stirrings of magic, nor did I feel I possessed any supernatural powers.

And Ember…if she hadn't met me, my mother wouldn't have known of her whereabouts. As soon as I'd touched Ember and we felt that connection, it was all my mother needed to know…

Mother. The word now sounded venomous to me. I'd never call her that again.

"It's my fault you're in danger now," I told Ember, trying to hide the waver in my voice. "My mother must have been watching my every move when I was in the human world.

When we touched and she saw the connection, she called the beast to mark you."

"Dawson, no," Ember said, as she swiveled in her chair and reached out for me. "None of this is your fault."

"Ember's right," Alex said. "If anything, it's ours." He glanced at Ember, his eyes burning with affection and sadness. "We're the ones who brought her into this world. Then your wolf fully awakened. If not for that—"

"It's not your fault either," Ember said firmly, making it clear she wasn't going to let any of us accept blame. "Eventually my wolf would've surfaced, whether I was brought into your world or not. I know that now. I've known since she emerged. I was the reason she'd lain dormant for so long. Not the world I lived in."

We sat in silence, our gazes locked on her. She wore an expression of determination edged in steel, and it took my breath away. As she surveyed the room, eyeing us one at a time as if to make sure we understood there would be no debating blame, Ravena's warning pierced the tension.

"Ember, please be careful. My sister is a strong halfling, probably the strongest I've ever known. She's uses her magic to get what she wants, but her wolf is equally determined."

Ember pursed her lips, deep in thought. "You took the necklace the night she gave it to me. What had Ciara done to it?"

"The necklace wasn't a gift. It was a curse," Ravena answered. "The longer you wore it, the weaker your wolf would've become. Eventually, you wouldn't have been able to shift at all."

Ember bristled. "Then once again, you saved my life. I owe you so much, Ravena."

Ravena shook her head in protest. "I should've forced my sister from this realm a long time ago, but I was afraid of her. She had the Alpha on her side, and the clan feared her just as much as I did…I didn't know what to do but try to undo some of what she'd done."

"But you can't remove the mark," Ember replied. It was a statement, not a question.

"I wish I could," Ravena told her. "But I'm not a dark witch. The most I could do was use a potion to help your wolf resist the call of the shadow creature. I wish I could do more."

"So, what do we do now?" Cody asked. "I hate sitting around like this when we could be doing *something*."

"We figure a way to remove the mark so Ember is free from the shadow realm," I said. I needed to make this right, to undo what my parents had done.

"Ravena," Alex said, stepping forward, an open book in his hands. "Do you recognize this?"

Ravena studied the page closely, her brow furrowed. "I've heard stories of this relic," she replied, as her fingers ran across the pages. "The person who possesses the eye of the moon holds great power over the shadow realm. Where there is darkness, there will be light. Souls will be released, and the lupus interfectorem realm sealed for eternity," she read.

"Wait," I said, stepping forward so I could take a closer look at the carefully drawn illustration. The circle with a smaller one nestled in the center wasn't an eye at all. I'd know that image anywhere. I'd been searching for that artifact for years.

"The moonstone," I revealed, all eyes now on me. "My grandfather wrote about it in his journal, but he could never locate it." I turned to Ember. "That's what I was doing in the human world. I believed it was there, but when I searched, I found nothing."

"We need to read your grandfather's book," Alex said decisively. "Maybe we'll find other clues in it that'll help us. If what this book says is true, and the bearer does hold control over the shadow realm, Ember could free herself from its mark. It may be the only way."

"She could also free her father," Cody added so quietly we almost didn't hear him at first, but his voice grew louder as though he'd figured something out. "She could release him from the shadow realm."

"What?" Ember asked breathlessly.

"In one of the books back in Thunder Cove, I found a passage that said there are two types of lupus interfectorem. One that—"

Ravena tried to stand up excitedly, but she didn't get far, her shackles clanging against the table. "Yes! This young man is right. There are hunters, and there are those who prevent captured souls from escaping." She nearly yanked the chains free, she was so animated. "Ember! You can save him! You can save Daniel!"

It didn't escape me this was the first time Ember had heard her father's name.

Daniel.

My former Alpha, a man who'd trusted my father with his life. Ravena had been right when she said he'd been a great leader and a man of honor who'd ruled with compassion and fairness. While I was too young to remember him myself when he disappeared, I'd heard many stories about him over the years. He'd left even bigger shoes to fill than my father had.

A man who should still be here, should still be Alpha.

The guilt I'd been carrying grew heavier as I once again thought about my father's confession. He hadn't said much in his final hours, but now that Ravena had told us the truth, it all made sense. I was crushed that my father had become so enraptured by the idea of power that he'd be willing to sacrifice an Alpha he'd loved so much.

I refused to be like him.

"And when we free Daniel, we'll restore him to his rightful place as Alpha of the Silver Creek clan," I said, as I reached out and took Ember's hands into mine. "I'll make this right. I promised you'd be happy and safe here. And I plan to keep that vow."

"Let's go examine the journal," Cody said impatiently. "Between the five of us, surely we'll find a clue that'll help us."

"Ravena," I replied, letting go of Ember's hands as I fetched a key from my pocket and crossed the room. "I'm grateful for everything you've done to help Ember. Please stay." I unlocked her shackles.

She looked up at me, rubbing her wrists. "Of course, I'll stay," Ravena replied, standing up and reaching over to hug Ember. "Silver Creek is my home. I wouldn't want to be anywhere else. But, Dawson, my sister must be stopped."

I didn't know what to say, but my heart knew what must be done, and the tears clouding my gaze spoke volumes.

There was only one thing I could do; banish my mother forever.

CHAPTER TWENTY-ONE

EMBER

I finally had the answers I'd been searching for. Though my mind was still trying to wrap around everything I'd learned as I walked with Grayson, Alex, and Cody toward Dawson's castle.

Dawson had told us he'd meet us later. And despite my asking if we could help, he'd shaken his head and insisted it was something he had to do on his own.

I couldn't imagine how he was feeling. Discovering his mother had conspired with his father to betray their Alpha, and that she wasn't who she appeared to be, had to be weighing on him. He'd looked so sad and lost when Ravena had told him. I only hoped his mother would leave peacefully, though I knew it was unlikely.

"I think we should go back to Thunder Cove right away," Grayson said as we turned onto another road and then cut through a nearby field. "I don't think being here is safe right now. We're better off being at home."

"I know," Alex replied. "But we need to see what's in the journal first. Perhaps there'll be information which will lead us to the moonstone. Then we'll head back."

I couldn't argue with them. It would be much safer in

Thunder Cove, especially knowing how evil Ciara was. The woman had sent a lupus interfectorem to murder my father and to mark me. I shivered at the thought of the monsters. Even though I was closer to finding a way to free myself from the shadow realm's grip, there was still so much to figure out.

My father.

All my life, I'd tried not to think about my parents, much less imagine I'd ever have a chance to meet them face to face. It had been safer not to daydream about such things. But when Cody told me the beasts kept the souls of their victims locked in the shadow realm and maybe this moonstone could help me break my father from those bonds, I hadn't stopped thinking about him—or daydreaming about meeting him.

I wondered what he looked like, how he'd feel about meeting me, and what kind of man he was. Ravena had spoken about how brave of a leader he'd been.

My mother.

She hadn't chosen to abandon me. All she'd wanted was to love her baby, but fate had stolen that from her.

My mind was a tangled mess of scattered thoughts. Guilt swelled inside over having ever believed my parents had self-ishly deserted me. Now I knew that couldn't have been farther from the truth.

I needed to unpack everything I'd learned, but I couldn't yet. I didn't have time to allow myself to fall apart. I had to find the moonstone, free my father, and remove the beast's mark.

Then I could give my heart a chance to break and then heal.

"Do you think Dawson should confront his mother on his own?" I asked the guys as we turned down the road which led to the castle. "Maybe we should've insisted on going with him."

"Absolutely *not*," Cody replied. "There's no way in hell we'd ever let you near Ciara again. She's the reason you're marked… the reason your father—"

"I know," I countered. "That's why I'm so worried. As Ravena said, Ciara is dangerous. What if she attacks Dawson? Uses her magic against him? She's his mother, but I don't know how far she'd be willing to go. I should've stood by his side the way he stood by mine."

"Ciara can't do anything to Dawson. He wouldn't confront her without alerting Craig and arranging for the royal guard to accompany him." Cody squeezed my shoulder affectionately. "So, please, don't worry."

Alex stroked the stubble on his face, deep in thought. "That's why she went after your father the way she did. Using dark magic to do her dirty work kept her hands clean. No one would've ever been able to trace it back to her if Ravena hadn't spoken up."

"And as Dawson said, he *needs* to do this on his own," Grayson added. "He's their Alpha. At least for now." He cleared his throat. "Dawson has a habit of running away from problems. This time he can't do that."

I wanted to ask what he meant, but I was too exhausted to open what could've been another Pandora's box of problems. In time, I knew I'd have to get to the bottom of whatever issues were between Grayson and Dawson. My heart demanded it.

We finally arrived at the castle, and I was thankful for it. I'd been running on adrenaline. As the events of the day caught up to me, I almost collapsed, but Grayson's strong arms wrapped around me.

"I've got you," he murmured as he hoisted me off my feet, cradling me in his arms as we made our way up the long drive. "I'm getting pretty good at this whole rescuing-a-damsel-in-distress thing."

I tried to say something sarcastic, but the words caught in my throat.

"Ember, we're going to find the moonstone," Cody reassured me as we entered the castle, and Grayson set me down. "And then you'll get to meet your father."

"There's a lot to do before we get to that," I replied honestly. I knew he was trying to lighten my spirits, but we didn't even know where the moonstone was, much less how it would help me find my father. I didn't want to get my hopes up.

"You're right," Alex agreed. "But we'll be with you every step of the way."

Tears welled in my eyes, but I blinked them back before they could escape. I'd been wrong to leave these loyal and loving men behind. Even though Silver Creek was my clan, and I had felt such a strong desire to be amongst my pack, I'd owed it to these men to have been honest with them, to have allowed them to say goodbye.

And now, as Alex wrapped his arms around me and held me tightly against his chest with the promise that they'd go on this dangerous adventure with me, I realized just how much I needed them, how I'd *always* needed them.

"When we get back to Thunder Cove, and you've had time to rest, I'd like to spend some time alone with you," Alex whispered into my hair. "Just the two of us."

"I'd love that," I replied. And I meant it. Alex always knew how to soothe my soul. Every touch was a reminder to breathe, to slow down. And I could use more of that in my life—more of him.

Grayson surveyed the sprawling foyer, a smirk on his face. "Such a big place. A little overkill, wouldn't you say? It looks like someone's overcompensating for something."

I wanted to laugh but thought better of it. Despite him rolling his eyes, there was no denying he was impressed by Dawson's home.

"I really do think we should head back to Thunder Cove and let Dawson come to us," Grayson added, looking around. "It doesn't make sense to stay here. I'd rather be home where I know our men will have our backs than leave my fate up to Silver Creek."

"I think we should give Ember a chance to catch her breath until Dawson gets here," Alex replied. "Then we need to look through his grandfather's journal. Maybe Dawson missed something which could lead us to the moonstone."

Grayson shot him a look which made it clear he just wanted to get the hell out of Silver Creek.

Before he could say anything, Cody spoke up. "I agree with Grayson. I don't feel safe here either." He stared up at a clock on the wall. "Maybe we should give Dawson an hour. If he isn't back by then, we'll leave him a note, and he can bring the journal to us."

"Sounds good," Alex agreed, finally releasing me from his embrace. "You happen to know where the kitchen is? Us wolves need to eat." He chuckled. "I saw a rabbit in one of the fields on the way here, and I swear to God, I almost shifted. I was so hungry."

I knew there was no way I'd be able to hold anything down with the way my stomach was rolling, but if Alex needed fuel, so be it. I led them toward the kitchen—one of the only rooms I could find my way to. Alex and Grayson got busy making dinner while I sat at the counter next to Cody. To my surprise and relief, the castle was empty with no housekeepers or staff present.

"How are you holding up?" Cody murmured to me as he poured us both a glass of lemonade. "I know it's a lot to take in at once."

"It is," I replied, taking a long drink to wet my parched throat. "But all I've ever wanted was the truth, and now I have it."

"And the truth shall set you free, right?" When he set his glass down, his mouth curved into something halfway between a smile and a smirk, making a blush creep up my cheeks.

"Well, technically, the *moonstone* will set her free, but sure," Grayson sniped as he sauntered over and topped up my glass.

His eyes found mine, and the smoldering gaze made me shiver from the heat. "Fuck, I've missed you."

He suddenly leaned over, dropping his arm across my shoulder, and I instinctively leaned into him, breathing in his masculine scent. This man was the storm and the shelter.

"And I've missed you," I replied, my voice shaking at the desperation in his. I peeked at Cody, then Alex. "I've missed all of you. I'm sorry I left the way I did. I promise I'll never do that again."

"Oh, you've got that right," Grayson murmured, easing away and giving me space to catch my breath. "Because now you know that if you do, we'll hunt you down."

I giggled. It felt good to laugh, to ease some of the pressure swirling in my chest.

"We heard so much about your old man when we were growing up," Grayson continued, taking a seat across from Cody and me. "When we used to come here to visit Dawson, people always spoke of the former Alpha. Plus, he and my father spent a lot of time together and even shared territory before the wars broke out again." He squinted his eyes, studying me as though he was seeing me for the first time.

"You kinda look like the photos I've seen of him."

"Really?"

"Well, kinda," Grayson answered. "Maybe just not as muscular, tall, or hairy."

I snorted. Count on Grayson to lighten the mood.

"Tell me about him," I said, leaning back and willing myself to calm down. "Tell me everything you ever heard."

Grayson spoke of my father's love of archery and fishing while Alex told me he had a penchant for games of strategy, particularly chess. I absorbed it all in until their words became whispers against a storm of dark thoughts racing through my mind, distracting me.

I looked up at the clock. Every minute that passed felt like an eternity. I needed Dawson to return home, so I knew he was safe.

"Dawson meant what he said," Grayson said, the mention of his name drawing me back to the conversation.

There was a flicker in Grayson's eyes which I couldn't quite read. "Your father will be Alpha of Silver Creek once again. Not that Dawson wanted the role anyway, but it rightfully belongs to Daniel."

Alex set a plate of food down in front of me, then leaned in and hugged me. The feeling of his arms wrapped tightly around me soothed my soul, and I didn't want the moment to end. "Try to eat something, Em."

"Thank you." I tried to do as he asked, but pushing food around my plate was the best I could do.

Cody noticed I wasn't eating and did his best to comfort me. "An Alpha's daughter," he murmured, reminding me that I came from strength, from a man who was born to lead. "Why am I not surprised? From the moment I saw you, I knew you were different." The words were deep and velvety, the sound of temptation.

Passion flared in his sparkling blue eyes, and the intensity of his steadfast gaze spread along my flesh like a lover's caress. He leaned forward, drawing me into his arms. Then his lips were on my mouth. The rest of the world was lost as he kissed me gently.

For a moment, I held back, but the sweet longing that rose inside me was too strong to resist. I leaned into his kiss, welcoming the reprieve from the many questions crowding my mind about the future. My body thrummed with desire for Cody, and my heart rejoiced at being back in his arms.

"We're going to get through this," Cody said as he eased back, his voice carrying a rough pitch of longing though I could sense he was trying to control it. "And then we've got a lot of catching up to do."

Footsteps behind me distracted me. When I turned, Dawson was leaning against the doorway, a curious smile playing on his lips. The look he gave me—the lift of his lips and one raised eyebrow—sent a flash of desire rushing through me.

"Are you okay?" I asked, embarrassed that he'd walked in on Cody kissing me. I felt selfish for sharing such a tender moment with another man while Dawson had been squaring off against his mother.

But his expression told me he wasn't bothered. I was confused, both by the devil-may-care look on his face and the fact he seemed to be way too relaxed for just having sparred with a ruthless witch.

"I'm fine," he replied as he reached for a bottle of whiskey and splashed some in a glass. But it was clear that he wasn't. "By the time I got there, Ciara was already gone. So was Richard." Dawson took a long drink and then refilled his glass. "She must have caught wind that her sister had confessed and knew she'd be banished."

When I gave him a look that told him it couldn't possibly be that easy, he shrugged.

"We have scouts standing watch at the portal, and Ravena is doing some sort of hocus-pocus that will prevent Ciara from reentering."

"And you're okay?" His mother had left his realm, and chances were, he'd never see her again. *Surely, he had to feel something?*

But when he gulped down another glass of whiskey, wiped his mouth with the back of his hand, and poured another, I realized perhaps what Grayson had said was true.

Dawson tended to run away from problems.

Did that mean he'd run from me?

"We need to look through that journal," Grayson reminded him, running a finger across the back of my hand. "After that, we're heading back to Thunder Cove."

Dawson's eyes flashed with hurt, before shuttering to blankness. "And you're going with them?"

I nodded as he raked his eyes over me, making me feel smaller than I already did. "I think it'll be safer for me there. For now.

"We need to find the moonstone. But I'll come back—"

"Yeah, of course. I completely understand," Dawson said with a shrug, dragging his gaze from my face to the whiskey bottle. "Let me bring you the journal so you can be on your way."

He shuffled out of the room, but I got up and followed him.

"Hey," I called out to him as he headed up the stairs. "Wait up."

He shot me a look over his shoulder and waited for me to catch up, then continued, moving slower than he usually would so I could stay next to him.

We walked in silence for several moments, the words I wanted to say stuck in the back of my throat. But as he led me into a large office, I finally found my voice.

"I don't feel safe here right now. With everything that's happened, I think the best thing is for me to return to Thunder Cove until I figure out what to do next."

His silvery eyes studied my face as though he could see through me. See beyond the make-believe bravery I hid behind, see beyond the marked girl who was so afraid she'd die before she ever had the chance to live.

As though he could see more than I could see.

"I won't stay away forever. When I've managed to free myself, free my father, we'll come back."

His silence was unbearable. I wished he'd say something— anything. Finally, he shook his head as if ridding it of unwanted thoughts.

"And how are you any safer there?" he asked me. His tone was gentle, his question an honest one. "The shadow realm can invade their territory just as easily, if they want to get to you. I guess I don't understand how leaving makes sense." His voice grew softer. "This is your clan, and we'll all fight for you. We'd never turn our backs on you, Ember."

"I know," I said truthfully, knowing there was no explanation which would make sense. Dawson was right; I'd receive no more protection in Thunder Cove than I would here, yet my heart longed to return. Now that I'd seen Grayson, Alex, and Cody again, I couldn't bear the thought of being separated from them.

"Anywhere I go, I bring danger with me. I brought it here, and there's a good chance I'll take it to Thunder Cove. I don't know whether I'm making the right decision, but it's where I feel I need to be. At least for now."

"I'd go with you," he replied, catching me off guard. "But I can't leave my clan right now. Not with everything that's happened. I hope you understand."

"Of course, I do." I nodded. "And I'd never ask you to leave them."

"No matter what, this is your home, and you'll always have a place here," he replied, his riveting gaze holding mine a moment longer before he turned away, unlocking what looked like a safe and riffling through its contents. When he turned to face me again, he held a worn, leather-bound book in his hands.

"I must have gone through this journal a hundred times searching for more information about the moonstone," he told me, flipping through the pages. "I thought it was hidden in the human world, but no matter how many places I explored, I couldn't find anything. I didn't realize what it was or how valuable. Maybe you and your guys will find something I've missed."

He peered at me, his jaw clenched. The way he'd referred to Grayson, Alex, and Cody as *my* guys wasn't lost on me. I wanted to tell him how much he meant to me and how much I wanted him to be a part of my life, just as much, but everything seemed so complicated.

It wasn't our time.

Perhaps it never would be.

He held out the book, and I took it into my hands, running my fingers over the soft hide, his eyes never finding mine.

"Take good care of it. It means a lot to me."

I furrowed my eyebrows in confusion. "No, Dawson. We can just look through it here before we go…see if there's anything—"

"I want you to have it. My grandfather wrote about all his travels. Some of his information may be useful on your journey."

I opened my mouth to protest, but he reached out, trailing a finger along my jawline.

"Nothing you say is going to change my mind," he added, his face breaking into a slow, sexy smile. "My grandfather loved your father, and I know he'd want you to have this."

I reached out and placed my hand flat against his chest. "Thank you. For everything."

He regarded me silently for a moment, his gaze running over my face like a loving caress. "Come on. I want to show you something."

He clasped my hand as we left his office and went back down the stairs. Rather than turn toward the kitchen, he led me in the opposite direction. As we rounded a long corridor, I recognized where we were. It was the same part of the castle I'd entered when he'd first brought me here just days ago.

As we made our way to the back of the castle, I suddenly knew what he wanted to show me. When he stopped abruptly in front of a large portrait, my heart soared.

"This," Dawson said, his tone hushed, velvety. "This is your father. Our Alpha."

I stared up at the painting, my eyes glued to my father's handsome face. He had dark brown hair, cut short on the sides, and a strong, square jaw. But it was the sparkle in his deep blue eyes which made me smile. I was certain whoever had painted his likeness had likely captured his very essence. As I looked up at him, I felt his energy—the unbreakable bond between father and daughter not even time, distance, or a monster from the shadow realm could break.

I had no conscious memory of this man, yet as tears streamed down my face, there was no denying my heart recognized him.

"When your father returns and takes his rightful place as Alpha, I hope you'll rule by his side. You'll be the most beloved princess our realm has ever known. Just as you are the greatest woman I've ever known."

Dawson's words took me by surprise, and when he reached for me, I let him pull me against his chest. His long fingers threaded through my hair, holding me still, as he peered down at me in the dim light, his eyes shimmering briefly in a muted flash through the windows.

Then he brushed his lips over mine, his kiss a mix of tenderness and barely controlled desire, bordering on rough. I wrapped my arms around his neck, drinking him in, returning his kiss with passion and fire of my own as though our bodies couldn't get close enough or taste enough of each other.

As though we might never get this chance again.

Far too soon, he broke away, taking his kiss with him.

"Come back to me, Ember," he whispered. His forehead rested against mine. His hands wound tightly around my waist as though I belonged to him. "When you're ready, please, come back to me."

He kissed my cheek, ever-so-softly. Then he released me before I could give voice to the words I so desperately wanted to say.

An ache speared through my chest as he walked away, but I knew I had to let him go. He glanced back at me one last time, his lips curving into a smile which told me more than mere words ever could before he disappeared around the corner.

I closed my eyes, wanting to commit his kiss to memory, the taste of his lips still fresh on mine.

When I opened my eyes and peered up at my father's portrait once again, tears streamed down my cheeks. I didn't know what the future held, or whether I'd ever find the moonstone that might set us both free, but I knew I'd never stop looking.

My mother had called me Ember because she'd believed I was the spark of hope for a better future.

I wouldn't let her down.

CHAPTER TWENTY-TWO

EMBER

I returned to the kitchen to find Grayson, Alex, and Cody waiting patiently for me. I lifted my hand, showing them the journal Dawson had given me.

"I'm ready to go."

They didn't ask where Dawson was, nor did they question my tearstained face. They seemed to sense I needed a moment, and I wasn't ready to talk.

Cody took my hand in his as we left the castle while Alex and Grayson led the way. As we strolled in silence, I took in the beauty of a realm that had felt like home from the moment I entered. The place I'd been born in, that my father had been Alpha of, and where my mother had taken her last breath.

I thought about Jasmine and how I wished I had the chance to say goodbye. She'd been a faithful friend to me, and I hated leaving this way. But I knew time was of the essence, and the sooner I left Silver Creek, the better.

A few minutes later, I felt the familiar warmth of the portal. The blinding blue light wrapped itself around me as I stepped through, my hand gripping Cody's tightly.

The thought of returning to Thunder Cove set my soul at

ease, though the idea of seeing Rylen again made my stomach turn. The last time I'd seen him, he'd attacked me, then told me I was a parasite who should be destroyed. The hatred that had burned in his eyes wasn't something I'd ever forget.

"There's something I have to tell you," I told Grayson, Alex, and Cody hesitantly.

Rylen was their beta, a trusted friend. The last thing I wanted to do was cause more trouble for Thunder Cove, but I couldn't go back without letting them know their right-hand man didn't want me there. There was no more room for secrets.

"When I was leaving Thunder Cove, I ran into Rylen. I was actually on my way back to find you so I could tell you that an army of men and wolves was coming." My words were barely a whisper, though my heart pounded so loudly it was like thunder in my ears. "And Rylen attacked me...threw me to the ground and made it clear I didn't belong there."

I felt the rage roll off Grayson's body, and he shook his head, fists clenched. "That mother fucker," he snarled. "He had no right to treat you like that."

I flinched at the fury in his voice, but Alex wrapped his arm around my shoulder. "Don't worry about Rylen," he said, though I felt the tension in his touch. He was just as angry as Grayson was. "We'll make sure he never hurts you again."

I caught the way Alex glanced at Grayson, and it was clear that he, too, was wondering how he'd control the fury begging to be unleashed on their beta. Cody tipped his head as though to let Alex know he understood—though what exactly, I didn't know.

It didn't take long before we were back at Thunder Cove, the warm, ocean breeze tickling my skin as we walked along the water, then cut through a meadow which would lead into town.

"My place or yours?" Grayson chuckled as he nudged me playfully.

The fire in his eyes told me that whatever rest I thought I'd get would be short-lived.

"Considering I'd been shacking up with you, you know the answer to that." I smirked, and he laughed again.

"You can have your pick of homes," Alex told me as we crossed the sidewalk toward his house. "Or we can always build you a new one."

"Or she could just live with me," Cody said, winking. "My place could use a woman's touch."

"It's not the only thing that could use a woman's touch," Grayson teased.

"I was hoping we could all stay together." I peered at Grayson from the corner of my eye, and I could see he didn't think it was such a bad idea.

"There's safety in numbers," he replied thoughtfully. "It makes sense for us all to stay together. And we'll let the clan know to be on guard as well. Hurry up. I can't wait to get you home."

He grabbed my hand and dragged me along while Cody and Alex shook their heads, huge smiles on their faces.

Grayson was many things, but patient certainly wasn't one of them. I couldn't help but giggle when he kept having to slow down because my shorter legs couldn't keep up. When we were just a few steps from the drive, he stepped in front of me and heaved me up over his shoulder like a caveman.

"Throwing me around is becoming your signature move," I told him as I dangled upside down against his back.

Alex reached for the journal, so I wouldn't drop it. "You *do* know that I'm capable of walking."

"But then I grab your ass like this when you're walking," he growled as he gripped a handful of my flesh.

A few minutes later, we were inside Grayson's room, six hands roaming my body, pulling at my clothes, tangling into my hair.

"Guys," I panted as I tried to find my voice to tell them we should go through the journal first, see what we might find.

But when Cody lifted my shirt over my head and Grayson stood behind me, his lips trailing kisses from my neck to my shoulder, all logic went out the window. My emotions led the way, and I gave in to my overpowering craving for these three men. In a flurry of flying fabric, the rest of my clothes and theirs found their way to the floor. I closed my eyes, surrendering to all the sensations engulfing me.

Soft lips painted my breasts with kisses, and when I turned to one, he held me only briefly before another greedily dragged me into his arms and ravished my body.

Grayson wrapped his hand around the back of my neck and yanked me forward a little roughly, sending a streak of fire across my breasts. "I've missed you so fucking much," he whispered hoarsely before his teeth grazed my throat, his bite gentle but firm.

Then he stepped forward, urging me backward, the sexy grin on his face telling me he knew *exactly* what he was doing. Though, for a moment, I was confused. Then I felt Cody's hard chest against my back, his arms snaking around to cup my breasts, squeezing them.

So, Grayson didn't mind sharing, after all.

"I missed you so fucking much," Cody told me, his deep voice rumbling against my cheek.

I closed my eyes, consumed by my need for these three men, my pussy thrumming as each took their time with me, switching from gentle and sweet kisses to hard, fiery kisses which bordered on savage.

"I need you," I moaned to no one in particular because the truth was, I wanted them all equally, but it was Alex who eased me into his arms, kissing my shoulders and my neck as we stumbled back together until the back of my knees hit the bed, and we tumbled onto it.

166

"And we need *you*," he answered, his perfectly sculpted body pressing against my bare breasts as his mouth claimed mine in a kiss which had me squeezing my thighs together in search of friction, my pussy so wet, so hot, so desperate to be touched.

Alex slid to my side, leaving my naked body exposed, readily available to be touched and kissed by all three men. Before I could blink, Cody had claimed my breasts, his hands squeezing each one. His tongue fluttered over my hard nipples, eliciting a whimper from me when he pulled one into his mouth and sucked.

I was panting by the time Grayson's hands traced down my stomach to my thighs, the smooth stroke of his skillful fingers nearly sending me over the edge. I spread my legs wider, my slit hot, wet, and wanting. I was theirs to do with as they wished, to use me for their own pleasure, to fuck me as hard and as long as they needed to.

My heart, body, and soul belonged to them and theirs to me.

"Fuck me…please."

I ached to be filled, to feel my pussy spread as it squeezed around Grayson's thick cock. But instead, I watched through bleary eyes as he eased down my body with an agonizing slowness, the kind which made me twitch and whimper. His amber gaze darkened before he lowered his head between my thighs. Each tantalizing kiss placed, almost strategically, along my flesh only served to torment me further, to rile me up with no hope of release in sight.

"Oh God, yes," I moaned, desperate to feel his lips where I needed them most.

The first flutter of his hot, wet tongue made me cry out, my hips thrusting upward, greedy for more. His finger slipped into my opening, stroking me inside as his lips tormented my pussy. Then he added a second finger, exploring my body, spreading me open, his skilled tongue never stopping, refusing to give me even a moment of respite even when I wriggled beneath him and cried out, "I'm going to come."

"Then come for me," he murmured, his tone commanding, as he continued to worship my pussy with his mouth and fingers. He was unyielding in his desire to make me fall apart, his tongue flickering over my clit, first lightly and slowly, then harder and faster, dipping just below before sliding back up. I shattered into a blinding orgasm, bucking against him as his thumb picked up where his mouth had left off, rubbing me, tormenting me with wild abandon.

"Yes…oh God," I whimpered as Alex squeezed the fullness of my breasts, while Cody raked his fingers through my hair, pulling my mouth to his.

Then Grayson nipped the tender flesh of my thighs, his teeth grazing my sensitive skin before his hands reached under me, squeezing my ass before flipping me over onto my stomach. "I need *more*, Ember," he whispered, his voice a gravelly, husky mess which did wicked things to my mind and body. "I need all of you."

"Then take it," I told him, thrusting toward him. "All of me. It's yours."

"And I'm yours." Grayson grabbed my hips and roughly pulled my ass against him, the thick head of his cock sliding against my ass.

And I wanted *more*. More of him. More of Alex. More of Cody. More of my gorgeous men, my powerful wolves. Being with them was electrifying, their hard bodies and soft mouths covering every inch of mine, needing me just as much as I needed them.

Cody slid down the bed, his cock brushing over my lips, but when I opened my mouth, eager to suck his length, the devilish grin on his face told me that wasn't what he had in mind.

Instead, he slipped beneath me so I was straddling him while

Grayson got behind me, pushing my thighs apart, the head of his thick cock dragging between my legs.

The mattress dipped for a moment as the three men jostled into position. Alex knelt in beside me, stroking his beautiful cock before pressing a finger over my lips, then two, wanting me to suck them, letting me know what he wanted me to do.

"I remember how beautiful you looked with a cock in your mouth," Alex murmured.

I'd never experienced anything like this before—the blissful pressure of a cock pressing between my thighs, sliding against my opening, while another pushed against my ass, and then Alex, stroking his cock in front of me, teasing me with it.

"Can I have this?" Grayson asked as he pushed the head of his cock against the cleft of my ass, pausing at the tight opening. "Can I have this part of you?"

I moaned my approval, his sexy words and the sensation of him rubbing slick fingers over my entrance, the only warnings given before I felt the wickedly punishing thrust as his dick squeezed inside me slowly, inch by inch.

I lurched forward as a deep, primal hunger drummed through my body, my pussy stretched and my ass tight around Grayson's cock. I'd never done this before, but my body willingly accepted him, inch by glorious inch.

For a second, I couldn't breathe, the sensation of being filled in both places so overwhelming, so satisfying, I could only cry out, my moans muffled by Alex brushing his cock over my open lips. His fingers tangled into my hair. I eagerly opened my mouth wider for him, wanting to taste and suck every inch of him.

"Fuck," Grayson growled as he gently slid his cock a little further into my ass, sending another thrill of pleasure through my body. "You make my cock so fucking hard."

Cody drove his hips forward, meeting mine, his hands snaking around my back, keeping me pinned against his chest while Grayson gripped my hips, his fingers kneading my flesh when he knew I was ready as he finally slid his full length inside of me. They worked together, in unison, filling me with so much pleasure I couldn't speak.

Incoherent thoughts rattled through my brain. My mouth sucked Alex's cock down deep and slow, coating it in my saliva, while my body continually thrashed against Cody's chest and then Grayson's.

"You feel so good…*too* good," Cody moaned, leaning up so his mouth could leave a trail of messy kisses over my breasts before burying his face between them. His hands snaked around my back, clutching my body, driving my hips down onto him as my pussy squeezed around him, the thrum of our motions, and the pressure from Grayson's cock an all-consuming force as I felt another orgasm building low in my stomach.

Then Alex cupped my face, my lips still tightly wrapped around his cock, and when I peered up at him, I recognized a gleam of barely controlled hunger in his emerald eyes. "I'm going to come, baby," he told me, his voice carrying the rough pitch of desire.

His hair fell into his face, but he pushed it back before returning his hand to the back of my head, his fingers tense. There was no mistake. He was now in control as he fucked my mouth.

"That's my girl. Don't stop, baby." The pleasure made his jaw clench as he watched me guide him through the stormy seas of desire. "Oh, God, Ember. Yeah, just like that."

Hearing Alex moan fueled me on as I sucked him deeper, flicking my tongue over the sensitive ridge and pumping his shaft with my hand, desperately wanting to give him as much pleasure as I could, his cock popping out of my mouth just long enough for my tongue to flutter over his balls, lavishing them with hot, wet strokes. Then I sucked him between my lips again.

Within seconds, he was moving restlessly, and I could feel

the pressure building, his cock throbbing against my tongue, and when he came hard and fast, I swallowed the sweet taste of his come.

Grayson pulled his cock from my ass slightly, leaving the thick head inside, pressing down on pleasure points I didn't know I had.

He was on the edge, right along with me, and when I ground my hips against him, I knew I'd pushed him to climax. He moaned, my name a whisper on his lips as his body shuddered and pulling all the way out, spilling his hot release on my ass. Cody's lips were back on mine, this time, his kiss fierce and desperate. A few seconds later, I broke away, rocking my pelvis against him as he thrust his hips upward, matching my rhythm, our bodies meshed together.

Then I was flying or falling, I didn't know, but the orgasm that rocketed through me left my body limp and tingly.

I let it all out then. Everything I'd been feeling for these three men came out in a warlike howl. All the frustration of having been away from them, the ache only they could fill, and above all else, the promise I'd never leave them again—it all came out in my strangled cry of release.

"Everything," Cody growled against my cheek, his voice rough, primitive, just this side of the powerful animal which lived within him. "You are my everything."

And with the next breath Cody took, he was falling right along with me, his body suddenly rocking hard against mine as his thrusts grew harder, faster, more insistent, and I clung to him, refusing to let go. In an instant, he slipped from me and gripped his cock, erupting in the space between us. His gaze locked on my face, his chiseled features strained as he clenched his jaw and rode out the final waves of his orgasm.

We lay together in a sweet silence for a few moments, catching our breaths and cuddling, until I managed to drag myself out of bed.

"Where are you going?" Alex mumbled lazily.

"To shower. You guys got me all sweaty."

Alex's lips curved into a sexy grin as he got up from the bed. "Come with me. I have an amazing tub in my bathroom. You can have a soak with me. Relax."

"Your tub isn't big enough for all of us," Grayson grumbled, his eyebrow cocked.

"Sorry, not sorry," Alex teased, holding his hand out to me. "You and Cody can hit the showers, so we don't have to share a bed with your sweaty asses. We won't be long."

What felt like moments later, Alex was easing me into a tub filled with steamy, lavender-scented water. My muscles sighed in relief as I sank below the surface. A second later, Alex settled in the massive, sunken tub behind me, his muscular chest tight against my back as his arms reached around me, a sponge in his hand.

"You know, this is the first time I've gotten you alone in so long. I think the last time was when we went for a walk together."

I thought about that night. I'd just woken after days of recovering from the first attack. It felt like a lifetime ago.

"That can't happen again," I breathed. "We need more time together. Alone time."

Alex dipped the sponge into the water, then slid it over my shoulders, leaving a streak of bubbles across my skin. It felt so good, too good, and my weary body sank into it, his gentle touch soothing as he proceeded to tenderly wash every inch of my body.

"I couldn't agree more. And this is a great start."

I felt the hot whisper of his breath, and as he dragged the sponge over my most sensitive areas, his lips pressed against my neck, right under my earlobe.

"Soon, we'll really make good use of this tub when I can take my time with you. But tonight, I know you're tired."

I started to protest, not wanting our time together to be over, but Alex chuckled as he rinsed me off.

"If we don't get back to the bed soon, you know they're going to crash our little party. Greedy bastards."

"I like the sound of next time," I replied huskily. "And next time, I'll wash your back instead."

I felt the curve of his smile against my skin as he lifted my hair so he could plant a kiss on the back of my neck—right where my mark was. It felt symbolic somehow, far beyond a simple kiss—as though he wanted to remind me that he didn't care about the danger I'd brought into his life. That he wanted to be with me, no matter what.

"You have yourself a deal."

Once we were clean and dry, Alex carried me back to Grayson's room, where he and Cody were already waiting for us. When I climbed back into bed, they wrapped me in their arms. "Sorry that was so quick, but it's what you do to us," Cody teased me, though his eyes glistened with the sincerity of his feelings. "We'll never get enough of you."

"Never," Grayson agreed, draping a hand over my stomach. "We're gonna need a bigger bed though."

Alex laughed sleepily. "It would be fine if you didn't hog the damn bed."

I smiled, then snuggled tightly against them. It was definitely a bit crowded, but I didn't care.

As far as I was concerned, I was in the only place I wanted to be.

CHAPTER TWENTY-THREE

EMBER

Grayson planted a kiss on my lips before he slipped out of bed, tugging on a pair of jeans.

"I'll be back soon," he whispered, not wanting to wake Alex and Cody, who'd fallen asleep moments ago.

I quirked an eyebrow. It was late, and we just had an amazing round of sex. Surely, Grayson was as tired as the rest of us?

But when he pivoted toward me again, now fully dressed, I could see it in the tightness of his jaw; he was a man on a mission. The dark glint in his eyes almost made me shudder. Then he was gone.

Suddenly, I knew where he was headed, and I also knew better than to try and stop him.

"Cody," I hissed, nudging him until he opened his eyes. "Grayson left. I think he's going to see Rylen."

He was instantly alert, understanding why I'd woken him, how afraid I was that Rylen might be more dangerous than anyone thought.

Cody raked his fingers through my hair, urging my head

closer so he could kiss my forehead. "Don't worry. I'll go find him."

I nodded as I watched him quickly get dressed. As he headed for the door, I whispered, catching his attention, "Should we wake Alex?"

Cody's head tilted, and even though his face was wreathed in shadow, I sensed this was something he felt he and Grayson should handle on their own. The thought scared me. Alex was the calm to their storm. Without him present, I feared Cody and Grayson might go too far. But I also knew I had to let them handle Rylen however they saw fit.

"I'll be back soon. Go to sleep, baby."

There was no chance I'd be able to rest until I looked through the journal, so I threw on Grayson's discarded shirt and trailed behind Cody, who was long gone by the time I made it downstairs with the book in my hands. I plopped down on the sofa, switching on the light next to me.

Thoughts of Dawson flooded my mind as I gazed down at the front cover of the journal. In the short time I'd known him, he'd captured my heart, and I knew there'd be no letting go. I hoped when I saw him next, I'd be returning to Silver Creek with my father.

Slowly, I thumbed through the journal, studying every page carefully. There were many illustrations of relics Dawson's grandfather had uncovered across this supernatural world and the human one. Drawings of rings, chalices, and golden statues graced the pages, along with details about where each item had been found.

According to the numerous handwritten notes about the Kingdom of Fire, the dragon realm was a place Dawson's grand-father seemed to have visited many times. Some of the entries were barely legible; the words were written haphazardly across the tops and bottoms of the yellowed pages as though he'd been so excited about his discoveries, he couldn't keep his fingers from trembling.

Dawson's grandfather also described how the dragons were mostly gentle creatures, despite their strength, though their population was dying, setting them on the verge of extinction. I remembered how Cody had told me that dragons were always welcoming to other shifters.

I continued poring over the pages, my heart thrumming in my chest as I read about the countless journeys Dawson's grandfather had taken. Some of his descriptions were so detailed I felt as though I was right there with him, exploring caverns, visiting realms, and uncovering ancient relics which had been lost for centuries. But there was no mention of the shadow realm. There was a sketch of the moon cycle which showed a half-moon every ten days, with a full moon rising halfway between each.

I flipped the page, reading and then re-reading each entry. I was halfway through the journal when a word jumped out at me, immediately capturing my attention.

Halflings.

Dawson's grandfather wrote about how halflings existed in every realm, though many lived in hiding, never revealing their true natures.

He penned stories about encountering half-dragons who could fly but couldn't breathe fire, as well as half-fae, who possessed powerful magic but couldn't easily control it.

Then, he wrote about half-humans, wolves who lay in slumber because they'd been away from their clans for too long, their beasts' powers fading with each passing day. Dawson's grandfather was gentle in his description of my kind, with no malice in his words, only a desire to understand.

I thought about the connection I'd felt when Dawson had first placed his hand in mine so many weeks ago at the carnival. As I read farther down the page, I realized it was likely the day my wolf had first awoken. According to an entry, the touch of a clan member was all it took to wake a sleeping wolf, and then they would find their way back home.

I thumbed through the remaining pages, stopping only when I reached the final entry. I stared down at the drawing of the moonstone, which looked exactly like the one Selena had found. Dawson's grandfather had written that it was one of the most powerful assets the Silver Creek clan could ever recover. And as Dawson had mentioned, it was last seen in an eastern town of the human world.

I took a deep breath, my heart heavy with the knowledge that while this artifact was the key to releasing the shadow realm's hold on me, and more importantly, finding my father, I had no idea where to find it.

There was only one page left in the bound book. The final entry was just a few lines about a broken moon and how dark creatures regenerated under the cracks of that moonlight.

A shiver crawled down my spine. There was no direct mention of the shadow realm or any connection to lupus inter-fectorems on the page, but I couldn't help but wonder if those were the dark creatures Dawson's grandfather had written about.

I searched my mind for information I felt was locked away, a thought that wanted to surface but was unreachable.

The night I was attacked in the human world as I made my way through the forest, I'd raced along the path, then moved to where the brush grew denser, seeking salvation in the shadows.

Then the day when the creature had attacked me in Silver Creek, I'd seen Ravena's silhouette standing by the path leading to the portal as she brought a gargoyle to life to help distract the beast.

Both times, a lupus interfectorem had come for me under a dimly lit sky, weaving through the darkness, waiting to strike.

Under the light of a half-moon, a *broken* moon.

I flipped back to the drawing of the moon cycle and counted the days, my heart thrumming with fear, my throat suddenly too tight.

If my hunch was right, it meant I had eight days to find the moonstone before the next attack.

Eight days before my life might be over.

CHAPTER TWENTY-FOUR

CODY

My body quaked with a rush of rage that blurred my vision as I strode down the pathway toward Rylen's place. I knew Grayson could handle him on his own, Rylen would never be a match for my Alpha, but I needed to see Rylen for myself, face to face.

My hands balled into fists as I quickened my pace. Knowing Rylen had attacked Ember as she tried to return home to warn us of Silver Creek's arrival heated my blood. The world around me started turning black. I tried to bring the fury down to a simmer, but it was impossible.

Not only had he robbed us of being able to say goodbye to Ember, but he'd put his hands on her and tried to break her spirit, to make her feel as though she was beneath us, that she wasn't worthy of a family, of a clan.

And for that, I needed to make him pay. Quietly, I slipped through his open front door.

My fist slammed into Rylen's bloody face before I spoke a single word. Grayson took a step back, stunned by my sudden appearance. Rylen countered my attack, hitting me back just as hard. We struggled against each other until I got the upper hand, smashing him against the wall, knocking over furniture, and nearly destroying a nearby bookcase as his fist pummeled my jaw. I returned blow for blow, my knuckles bleeding and my vision blurring as pure adrenaline took over.

"Don't you *ever* put your hands on Ember again," I growled in between cracks to his face, each swing punctuating the anger that bled through my veins. "You are not what Thunder Cove stands for." I blasted him with another punch, trying to knock the smirk off his face.

"I was only doing my job," Rylen bit back as his fist cracked the wall behind me when I sidestepped him. "Silver Creek wants her...let them deal with her." Another missed punch split the wall behind us, leaving a hole the size of his fist.

"You're the one who told Silver Creek Ember was here," I snarled, finally understanding how it came to be that the clan even knew Ember was in our realm. "And then you handed her over like she was livestock."

Rylen grabbed the collar of my shirt and tried to maneuver me into a corner of the room, but I jerked away, landing another crack to his face.

"She's a halfling," he gritted back, his mouth bloody as he took another swing, punching my stomach with such force it almost knocked the breath out of me. "Livestock holds more value than she does."

Hearing him speak about Ember that way made my wolf howl to be free, to sink his fangs into Rylen's flesh and end his life. I fought against the urge to shift, though I was quickly losing control.

Grayson pushed me out of the way and grabbed Rylen by the throat, slamming him against the wall. "If you ever speak of Ember that way again, I'll rip your throat out." His grip tightened as Rylen stood in stunned silence. "Do you understand me?"

Something in Rylen's expression suddenly changed. A realization seemed to hit him like a freight train, and he almost slumped to the floor when Grayson let him go.

"You're in love with her," Rylen said, his voice cracking in disbelief. "All of you...you're in love with the same woman. You put a halfling over the safety of our clan."

"Don't ever fucking question my loyalty to this realm," Grayson snarled, his voice filled with warning. "I would die for my pack." He stared Rylen in the eye as though he needed to make sure his point was clear. "And I would die for Ember."

It didn't matter that Ember was a halfling or that she wasn't part of our clan. Grayson was in love with her, and nothing—not Rylen, not anyone—would stand in the way of that.

"Is she your fated?" Rylen asked, spitting blood onto the floor and wiping his lips with the back of his hand. "Is that what you're saying? That Ember is your fated mate? If so, how can that be if Alex and Cody are also in love with her?"

For a split second, the anger in Grayson's eyes faded just slightly as he stared down Rylen, the complicated question lingering between them. It was the same question which had been burning in my mind, the fear of losing Ember dominating my every thought.

I'd already come to terms that if she chose either Grayson or Alex as her mate, I'd stand by her, be whatever she needed. Ember deserved happiness, and I wouldn't let my selfish desire for her stand in the way of that.

But when Grayson failed to admit Ember wasn't his fated mate, and that while he had strong feelings for her, she wasn't his to claim, my heart dropped to the floor, as did my gaze.

If Grayson declared he wanted Ember to be his lifelong mate, I'd never be able to kiss her again, taste her skin, or feel her in my arms. I wished I could talk to Grayson and Alex about it...but as their beta, I knew I'd have to accept whatever they decided.

An Alpha's mate was untouchable, belonging only to him. And him to her.

"She's staying," Grayson replied, refusing to answer the question. "And if you can't accept that…if you can't treat her with the same respect you treat me, then pack your bags and leave this realm. Because if you so much as look at her sideways, there'll be hell to pay."

Rylen shook his head slightly, his expression suddenly unreadable.

"She's back?" he stammered. "You brought her back here?"

"We did," I answered, my jaw clenched. I silently dared Rylen to fight us on this, to say another damning word about how Ember didn't belong in Thunder Cove, but he said nothing. Then his shoulders slumped, and it was apparent he understood that he either accepted Ember or he'd be rejected by his clan.

"But she's marked," he whispered, his voice low, weak. "Which means the shadow realm will attack us again if she's here."

"We've learned more about the shadow realm," Grayson told him, his fists still clenched. "We need to find the moonstone. Then we can remove the mark."

I leaned against the wall, catching my breath, but I shot up when Rylen advanced on Grayson, his eyes wide.

"I know where it is," Rylen said, his jaw tight. While he still wore a hardened expression, he started to nod, his dark eyes distant and reflective. "The moonstone…I know where it is."

The expression on Grayson's face was one of mistrust, as though he couldn't bring himself to believe Rylen might hold the answers.

"What do you mean, you know where it is?" Grayson fired back, leaning forward and closing in on Rylen's space. "Bullshit."

Rylen nodded tiredly and squared his shoulders, his face the most serious I'd ever seen. "It's in the dragon realm."

Grayson's eyes sparked with anger, the rumors we'd heard

suddenly confirmed. Years ago, there'd been murmurings of how Rylen sold relics discovered by wolves to other realms in exchange for gold. When confronted, he'd denied it, and the rumors had stopped.

I watched in silence as the fire in Grayson's eyes burned even brighter as he realized his beta had withheld information which Ember so desperately needed.

"Which dragon realm?" Grayson's voice was a deep rumble, the sound of a man on the verge of murder.

Rylen hesitated, and Grayson's temper flared as did his impatience. He lunged forward, grabbing Rylen by the throat and pinning him against the wall. "Which dragon realm? I won't ask again."

The way Rylen's dark eyes refused to meet Grayson's, even with his Alpha's hand squeezing the breath out of him, was the only answer we needed.

Most dragon realms welcomed other shifters and were led by strong and honorable Alphas. The dragon realm I'd visited out of sheer curiosity as a young man had received me with open arms.

But not this one.

The realm in question—the name still stuck on Rylen's tongue as Grayson's grip tightened—welcomed no one.

That realm had been destroyed by its own fire and ash. The clan was led by a ruthless dragon who'd murder every shifter alive if it meant he was the most powerful—the most feared Alpha of them all.

Bloodstone.

The realm that had murdered Grayson's father.

CHAPTER TWENTY-FIVE

EMBER

I opened my eyes and found myself deep in a tangle of legs and arms. Alex's hand was draped across my stomach, and Cody nuzzled against my side.

Somehow, after falling asleep on the sofa with the journal on my lap, I'd been brought to bed without stirring me. It wasn't a surprise. My emotions had been put through the gamut. My mind and body had been beyond exhausted.

I peered around the room from my limited vantage point, seeking Grayson, but as I carefully squeezed out from the Alex-Cody sandwich and slid down to perch on the end of the bed, he entered the room with nothing but a towel wrapped around his waist.

"Good morning, sweetheart," Grayson murmured, his voice raspy, as though he was exhausted.

I wondered if he'd even slept. Before I could ask, he leaned over and planted a kiss on my mouth.

"Good morning," I replied, all smiles. "You're up early. Did you even sleep?"

Grayson raked his fingers through his wet hair, his tired eyes answering my question as to whether he'd even slept. He turned his attention to the nearby closet as he searched for something to wear. When I asked again, he shook his head.

I frowned as I watched the muscles ripple across his back. Jagged lines of puckered flesh marred his skin. They were reminiscent of the marks I'd seen on Dawson. Now wasn't the time to ask Grayson about it.

"I don't need a lot of sleep," he assured me, trying to ease my mind.

Alex stirred behind me, and then his eyelids fluttered open, though it took him a few seconds to come fully awake.

"Well, at least one of you slept well," I said as Alex's lips curved into a sexy grin, which told me yes, he certainly had.

"Like a baby," he replied with a sleepy smile, scooting over to sit next to me, his palm sliding down my thigh, fingertips fluttering over my skin. "I have *you* to thank for that."

The fire in Alex's touch made me drowsy with desire, and it took all the willpower I had to slip away, even when he slid down next to me and tried to wrangle me back under the sheets.

"Make that two of us," Cody murmured, his eyes cracking open just slightly before he rubbed at them, shielding himself from the beam of sunlight which highlighted his handsome face. "Where are you off to? Come back to bed."

"I need to keep searching," I told them all. "I read through the journal last night, and I didn't find much. One thing stood out to me, though. I think it's possible the moon holds a lot of influence over the shadow realm."

Grayson raised an eyebrow. "Everything in the world is influenced by the moon in one way or another."

I filled them in on what I'd read and how the journal mentioned that dark creatures regenerated only under the cracks of moonlight. Then I explained how both times I'd been attacked, it had been under a half-moon.

"Perhaps they can't leave their realm unless it's a half-moon,"

Alex murmured, mostly to himself. "Or maybe that's when the portals are open to them, or simply when they're at their strongest. So many things we don't know yet."

Grayson wrinkled his nose as though it wasn't making sense to him. "And why would the shadow realm only send one beast at a time? Why not send an army of them to get the job done?"

That same question had been on my mind since the creature had attacked me. I'd narrowly escaped the attack of one creature at a time. There was no way I would've survived more than one.

"Maybe it's because they *can't*," Grayson replied, answering his own question and dropping the towel to his feet.

I couldn't look away, my eyes glued on his sinfully gorgeous frame, a perfect column of hard muscle and tanned skin.

"Huh?" I choked out, lost in fantasy.

Grayson dipped his chin to stare me in the eyes, his dark hair tumbling across his forehead in a sexy, wet mess. "I said maybe it's because they can't." His lips curved into a sensual grin when he'd caught me gawking.

"Oh, right," I replied, my cheeks flaming. "I sure hope that's true. The idea of more than one of those is terrifying."

"I wish we knew more about the shadow realm. It would certainly make it easier to come up with a solid plan," Alex added thoughtfully.

"About that," Grayson told us, finally dressed and sitting down next to me. "We know where the moonstone is."

We know where the moonstone is.

The words echoed through my mind, the sweetest sound.

I smacked his shoulder playfully. "And you're just telling me this now?" I stammered, my body tingling with relief and my heart hammering in my chest.

We were one giant step closer to figuring out a way to release my father.

"Grayson, we'll be able to save my father!"

His eyes darkened, making it clear that with the good news

came some bad. He reached for me, practically pulling me onto his lap, his arms wrapped around me.

"What is it? What's wrong?"

Grayson and Cody exchanged a glance while Alex seemed just as confused as I was.

"Please tell me," I demanded impatiently, my voice quavering. I sat up a little straighter, sliding off Grayson's lap. "Where is the moonstone?"

Something shifted in his gaze, causing my pulse to spike, though I didn't know why.

"It's in a dragon realm. A place called Bloodstone," Grayson finally revealed, his tone calm and even, though his expression was anything but. "It'll be a challenge to convince them to give it up."

Alex moved next to me, his calm energy washing over my body, helping to settle my nerves.

"We'll get the moonstone," he reassured me when I fell silent. He looked over to Grayson, his eyes filled with a deep sadness as he rested a hand on his friend's shoulder. "If we have to fucking destroy Bloodstone to get it, so be it. It's long overdue."

I peered out of the corner of my eye at Alex, his words so out of character they left me stunned.

Then something lifted, and the tension rolling off Grayson's body faded as he squeezed me against his chest, and whatever was bothering him was forgotten.

At least for the moment.

I padded into my bedroom wearing Grayson's t-shirt, which hung to my knees. I was desperate for a hot shower and a clean set of clothes. But as I entered my room, I froze, my eyes glued to the large box on my bed.

Intrigued, I searched for a note or card—*anything* to indicate who it was from, but there was none to be found.

I turned when I heard footsteps behind me and found Grayson leaning against the doorframe, a sly grin on his face.

He nodded. "Go ahead and open it."

I fidgeted as I fingered the pretty, red paper, then peered back over my shoulder when Grayson closed the distance.

"Are you one of those annoying people who takes their sweet time unwrapping gifts?" he teased, tearing a strip of the paper.

I grinned. He had me pegged. I hadn't received many presents in my lifetime, so I tended to savor the opportunity. I could spend an hour unwrapping a gift, wanting to make the experience last for as long as possible.

"I sure am." I laughed. "Unwrapping is half the fun."

I gently ripped the paper, peeling back the front of the package as colors peeked out. I had no idea what I was looking at, but as I stripped off another piece, my excitement growing, I couldn't stop the sob which escaped my lips when I realized what Grayson had done.

"I was hoping for smiles, not tears," Grayson murmured as he stood behind me and wrapped his arms around my waist. "I know it's a bit early, but happy birthday, Ember."

I stared at the gift through the blur of tears. No one had ever given me something so meaningful before. So incredibly heartfelt. So personal.

I reached out, removing the last of the wrapping. Sitting on the bed in front of me was a large painting. A blend of earthy colors formed a boardwalk while streaks of pinks and blues shimmered in the backdrop just above a turquoise ocean which sparkled like diamonds. And standing on the sandy bank was a woman, her hair a blend of chestnut and gold wearing shorts and a t-shirt.

"That was the day," Grayson murmured as he nuzzled his chin against my shoulder. "That was when I knew."

I closed my eyes as his hot breath tickled my collarbone. His lips brushed over the crook of my neck. I wanted to stay in this moment forever.

"We'd gazed out at the ocean. You said Thunder Cove was a captivating place. Yet you were all I could see." He shifted me toward him.

His amber eyes lit with a steady fire I hadn't seen before. It wasn't just a look of desire or the heady glint of a man with one thing on his mind. It was something different, something far more meaningful. "You are the most captivating woman. The only woman I see."

His eyes were filled with so much emotion I found myself speechless, mesmerized by the gorgeous man who held me, entranced in his spell.

"That's when I knew, Ember." He leaned forward and pressed his cheek against mine, his lips softly brushing across my skin. His gaze was so intense, his kiss so tender, that I almost forgot to breathe. "That's when I knew I was in love with you."

My eyes welled with tears I couldn't blink away. Grayson ran his thumb over my cheek, collecting them as they fell.

"And I will *always* love you."

I melted against the heat of his body, his words setting my heart ablaze. And when he brushed his lips against mine, the hunger on his breath made my knees go weak. I leaned into him for support.

"Grayson," I whispered into his hard and possessive kiss. I'd been wanting to say the words to him for so long but hadn't ever dared. "I love you too."

His smile deepened, and the hunger in his eyes grew more intense, as did his kiss.

By the time he let me go, we were both breathless, our need for one another so strong it took everything for us to tear ourselves away.

There'd be plenty of time for kisses. Though even forever with Grayson, Alex, and Cody wouldn't be long enough.

Grayson seemed to have other plans. His gaze flicked to my mouth and then slowly made its way up my face. "After all of this is over, we're taking a long honeymoon."

I quirked an eyebrow. "Honeymoon? But you haven't even proposed yet."

"True," he agreed softly. "But I *have* carried you over the threshold a time or two."

"I think you'll have to do a little better than that." I laughed. "Besides, since when are you a marrying kind of guy?"

"Since I met you," he replied. "But don't think I'm going to be one of those dudes who gets all soft and mushy when they're in love. *Not* going to happen."

I laughed. "Oh, honey, I think that ship has sailed."

"Well, keep it between us." He smirked, but the playfulness in his expression suddenly faded. "You know, Alex and Cody are in love with you too. Maybe just as much as I am." His gaze slid from mine. "It's going to take me some time. You know, to get used to that." After a brief pause, he continued, "But if they make you happy, that's all that matters to me. I just need you to know that sometimes I'm going to be selfish and want you all to myself."

Before I could begin to consider the significance of his words, he settled his mouth on mine, robbing me of coherent thought. His hands slid down to circle my waist, cupping my ass, drawing me hard against him, his hips flexing just slightly.

"So, back to planning our honeymoon," he murmured, and I felt the shape of his smile against my lips before he stepped back just slightly, his gaze lowering to my breasts. "Think we could get a head start on it?"

I snickered. "I don't think we have time for that."

"Come on, baby." His smile went all dark and sexy around the edges, his golden eyes fixated on me.

This was a man who knew *exactly* how to use all the sexy weapons in his arsenal, and he had many. I stared at his gorgeous mouth, slightly parted, waiting for me.

"We can make time." Gently, he tossed me onto the other end of the mattress. My head had barely hit the pillow before he'd whisked his masterpiece over to the corner and levered his body over mine. "There's always time to love you."

I moaned as he pinned me to the bed, his fingers already at work as he lifted my shirt over my head. Then, the hot, wet trail of his tongue slid over my skin, from my neck to the tip of each hard nipple, and I gave in.

He was right. There was time.

There was *always* time for each other.

CHAPTER TWENTY-SIX

EMBER

I made plans to see Selena to say goodbye while Grayson, Alex, and Cody headed out to meet with the clan so they could bring them up to speed on everything that had happened.

When I'd voiced my concern that Thunder Cove would be left defenseless with both Alphas gone, Grayson reassured me they had plenty of men who'd protect the realm while we were away, though I noticed how he didn't mention Rylen's name.

It also didn't escape me that both Grayson's and Cody's knuckles were swollen.

Dark thoughts plagued my mind when I contemplated how much they were risking for me.

"We do this together," Grayson insisted, his voice tinged with that fierce baritone rumble which set my heart aflame. He pulled my hands into his. "Or not at all."

I glanced down to where we were joined, then nodded. I didn't seem to have a choice.

"Together."

A few minutes later, I was knocking on Selena's door.

She nearly ripped it from its hinges; she was so excited to see me.

"I want to thank you," I told her after she'd finished squeezing the breath out of me. "It's because of you that I even know about the moonstone. I can't thank you enough, Selena."

"Please be careful, okay? The Bloodstone realm isn't like ours," she replied, her expression somber. "And their Alpha, Jericho, is one of the most ruthless dragons alive."

I got the sense she wasn't telling me half of it, but then she changed the subject, an apparent attempt to lighten the mood.

"I met someone," she continued wistfully, twirling her hair around her fingers. "I can't believe I'm saying this, but I'm madly in love—absolutely obsessed."

"Selena! That's wonderful! Tell me about him."

She bit her lip for a moment, fighting her giddy smile, then nodded. "We met on the night of the Fallen Moon, drawn to each other across realms. As soon as we touched, I knew he was the one." Her cheeks turned rosy, and she couldn't seem to stop smiling. "But enough about that, I don't want to make this all about me. Not when you're getting ready to leave. Come here, I need another hug."

I thanked her again before I said goodbye, promising I'd let her know the minute I returned to Thunder Cove. Then, I met up with Grayson, Alex, and Cody, watching while they finalized plans, which included intently studying a map of the Bloodstone realm.

"I wish we could take our whole army with us," Cody muttered.

"Me too. But you know how paranoid Jericho is about outsiders. He'd definitely see it as an act of aggression," Alex said.

"Jericho has watchtowers inside the portal," Grayson explained. "Scouts who guard the entrance around the clock. We won't be able to go in undetected, so we need to prepare for that. Remember, the important thing is to stay together. Always."

"I wish Ember would stay behind," Alex said to Grayson and Cody, as though I wasn't standing right next to him. He caught the quirk of my eyebrow and placed a hand on my shoulder. "I know you want to find the moonstone, but you should stay here, where it's safe, while we retrieve it for you."

"That's *not* happening," I replied firmly. "Besides, I wouldn't be any safer here. I won't be safe *anywhere* until I defeat the shadow realm. This is my problem. Not yours. I'm still struggling with the fact you're coming with *me*."

Alex and Cody exchanged a look that left me unsettled.

"Is there something you're not telling me?" I asked them. "I want to think we're above keeping things from one another at this point."

A troubled expression crossed Grayson's face as he gazed at me sideways, but it was gone a second later. "When Jericho waged war on other shifter clans, it wasn't for wealth or territory. It was for our women."

I looked at him, jaw dropped, speechless.

"The dragon population is on the decline," Alex added. "Jericho thought stealing other women would solve their problem."

His words shook me to the core, but nothing was going to keep me from entering the realm of dragons. I needed the moonstone to free myself from the control the shadow realm had on me, and I wouldn't let anyone else—especially not three men I adored—fight that battle without me.

"Jericho *will* give us the moonstone," I told them, hoping my shaky voice didn't betray me. I needed to be strong, to reassure them I wouldn't back down. I'd already stared death in the face and survived. *Twice.* Not even a brutal dragon was going to stand in my way of saving my father and myself.

They seemed to understand there'd be no argument, though Alex peered at me intently, his eyes flickering as though he hoped I'd change my mind. When I didn't, he sighed. "If you insist on going, there's something I want you to have." He left the room only to return a few minutes later. In his hand, he held a small dagger, the handle and sheath adorned with colorful jewels.

"I don't—"

He shook his head to silence me. "I'd feel better knowing you had this on you. For protection." Finally, some of the somberness in his expression lifted, and a tremble of a smile played on his lips. "It was my mother's. When she was young, she was a force to be reckoned with. She'd bring this with her when she traveled outside the realm."

I accepted it and turned it over in my hands. "Thank you," I replied. "It's gorgeous."

"It's also very sharp," Cody added. "Be careful with it."

"I don't know how to use it," I replied. "Any tips?"

"If a bad guy comes near you, jab it into him and run," Grayson chuckled.

I laughed despite the fear in my heart at what was to come. "Got it."

An hour later, as we crested a hill with the sun at our backs, I peered over my shoulder at the beauty of Thunder Cove.

This world I'd been brought into was so different from the one I'd grown up in, but even with danger at my heels, it had made me feel safe. Like I belonged.

And so did the men who surrounded me, their love fueling me with the strength I needed to go on. To never give up.

I took a long moment to take it all in, to reflect on all I'd discovered about myself. When Grayson and Cody pulled me into their arms while Alex stroked my hair lovingly, I knew I'd made the greatest, most powerful discovery of all.

I'd learned to believe in myself.

And I'd learned to believe in love.

I nodded, signaling I was ready to leave this realm for the

next, that I'd fight with everything I had in me to be free of the shadow realm because then I'd be free to be with them.

A lifetime of possibilities lay in front of us. We just had to fight for it.

"We can do this," Cody told me, gripping my hand in his. "We *will* do this."

And I believed him.

But as we made our way toward the edge of Thunder Cove's territory, I thought about another man who'd never fade from my memory, no matter how much time may pass between us.

Dawson.

His name echoed through my heart like a drum, the sound steady and sure, getting louder with every beat.

Our connection was deeper than merely being from the same clan. Dawson had captured a piece of my heart as well. In such a short time, we'd discovered a bond which was strong, unbreakable. He'd welcomed me home even when we'd known little about my past.

And when he'd kissed me under the moonlight, my heart had split in two, part of it in Thunder Cove and part of it in Dawson's hands.

Grayson chuckled softly, a sound I could listen to for the rest of my life. When I peered at him, he was looking straight ahead, his gaze fixed on something off in the distance. I followed his line of sight as a lone figure came into view, wearing a smile brighter than the sun, and it took my breath away.

This beautiful man had come for me once, and now, he was here again. My heart seemed to believe he'd never left.

"Dawson," I whispered in disbelief. "You're here."

He took a moment before he stepped forward, confusion mixed with relief, his gaze locked on mine.

"We'll fill you in on everything," Grayson told him, his expression one of patience and acceptance.

Patience that whatever history the two of them shared

would be dealt with after we'd won this war together—side by side.

And as Grayson, Alex, and Cody stepped back, giving me and Dawson a moment alone, I saw the gleam of acceptance in their eyes. They knew how much Dawson meant to me, and they believed somehow, we'd find a way to make it work.

I stepped forward, and Dawson drew me into his arms, pressing his hard body against my curves. I felt the muscles in his arms and shoulders as my fingers moved over him, and when he pulled me even closer, I felt his hardness.

He eased back so he could peer into my face. "I have something for you. Ravena found this." Dawson dipped his hand in his pocket and pulled out what looked like a small piece of paper. "She wanted you to have it."

My eyes darted down to his hand and as he held it out. I realized it was a photograph, the edges worn.

"It's your mom," he whispered.

With trembling fingers, I took the image and studied it through tear-filled eyes. My mother was beautiful, her expression youthful and her eyes filled with warmth. But there was something else, something far greater than her beauty and as I stared lovingly at her photo I suddenly knew what it was.

I had never had the chance to know my mother, nor had I ever felt her arms wrapped around me, yet my heart recognized her immediately. The bond between a mother and daughter, one so natural, so powerful, that even death couldn't break it.

"You have her smile," Dawson murmured, pulling me from my thoughts.

I wanted to spend hours staring at her face, but I knew time wasn't on our side. With one final glance at the woman who'd given me life, I tucked the photograph in my pocket, careful not to bend it. I blinked to clear my vision.

"Thanks for bringing this to me, Dawson."

Dawson tugged me back into his arms. "Ember, wherever

you're going, I'm coming with you," he told me, his embrace tightening as he pressed his lips to mine. "I want to be there for you. Every step of the way. Fighting by your side." The way his mouth tipped up hinted that he had more to say, something on his mind, but for now, it could wait.

"Are you sure?" I asked him. I wanted him to join us, of course, but I knew that just like Grayson, Alex, and Cody, he was risking so much.

"I've never been surer." His voice was threaded with steely determination. "I don't care what I have to do. I'm never walking away from you again."

I had no idea what fate awaited us once we'd crossed into the dragon realm, but as I followed my lovers toward the unlit portal—a stark contrast to the warm, blinding light of Silver Creek's entrance—I knew I'd never be alone again.

"There it is." Cody's eyes blazed. "Are we ready?"

"As ready as we'll ever be," Alex replied.

I noticed how he glanced at Grayson. A flash of hurt flickered on Grayson's face before he smothered it with a tight smile.

"Together," he said, echoing his words from earlier after Alex whispered something to him I didn't quite catch. "We do this together or not at all."

Grayson took my hand in his, charging at the portal with Alex, Cody, and Dawson right behind us. My stomach was in knots as we stepped into the mix of smoky mist and a flush of dusky light. I clung on to Grayson for dear life, as step after step we walked. The portal felt endless and my heart thudded with fear that we were trapped.

Then I saw it, the swirl of fire and ash on the other side of the portal. After another step forward, the gray fog made way for sparks of light.

But as soon as we stepped foot inside the Bloodstone realm, the stench of death rose, and I sputtered, struggling to breathe.

Dawson covered his face with his arm and tugged at my elbow. "So this is where we turn around, right? Because—"

A sudden lurching of the ground caught us off guard, sending us toppling toward a disgusting cesspool of brown and green vileness. I caught myself just before the tip of my shoe slipped and touched the edge of the strange mass.

The rubber hissed and curled inward on itself, smoking a sulfur-like stench into the already putrid air, and I kicked it off, scrambling back.

"Get back!" Cody yelled, but he was a second too late.

In horror, I saw Grayson falling face-first right into whatever it was.

The last word I heard on his lips was my name, and my heart raced up into my throat. It was a desperate cry for help, and despite how stepping forward promised a painful death, I knew I'd do anything to save him.

ABOUT CATE CASSIDY

Cate Cassidy is an '80s movie buff who is addicted to coffee and tales of magic and mayhem.

Fun fact: She's watched *Teen Wolf* a dozen times and *Lost Boys* more times than she can count. #DeathByStereo

Cate lives near the ocean in Atlantic Canada with her attention-seeking Bengal, Darwin, who occasionally moves off the keyboard long enough for her to write a chapter or two.

Printed in Poland
by Amazon Fulfillment
Poland Sp. z o.o., Wrocław
23 September 2021

ac931d69-dc46-4a9f-bc4a-dc01527e8ddbR01

—